I0614423

SAVED BY GRACE SERIES 2

2nd Edition

THE STORY
OF
WADE...

The Road From Darkness To Redemption

Dr. AudreyAnn C. Moses

OTHER BOOKS BY DR. MOSES

Kelly Crews Publishing

The Swing (2018)

Uninvited Memories (2018)

Saved by Grace: Walking Through Affliction Into

God's Deliverance (2017)

Voice of Truth Publishing

RITES OF PASSAGE:

Does It Give American Black Youths the "Right To

Pass?" (2010)

(Assisted by Kenneth Nyamayaro Mufuka, Ph.D.)

DEDICATION

This book is dedicated to…

All of us who, for various reasons, are (or have been) tormented by The Voices, while we lived in our darkness.

To the Mental Health Professionals who help guide us out of our darkness.

And to our families that pray day and night, asking for a Divine intervention to bring us out of the darkness, putting us on the Road to Redemption and a new life.

2 Timothy 2:7 (KJV)

Hebrews 13:5 (KJV)

ACKNOWLEDGMENT

*Thank you, God, for helping me to do something I've always done in private,
but now I can do it public – write.*

I would like to thank all of the wonderful people that God has put in my life, specifically to help me write. One more time, my personal editor, Valerie Baty painstakingly read the first draft, full of my voice with many errors and turned it into something legible for others.

Thank you to my husband, Leonard and my sons, LJ and Stefan (and families) who are my best encouragers.

And, thank you, Saved By Grace fans who insisted there was more to Wade. So once again, thank you for trusting that **The Story of Wade** *is worth your time to read.
Enjoy!*

"Dreams do not come to life independent of others..."

TABLE OF CONTENTS

PROLOGUE

"Some become fools through their rebellious ways and suffered affliction because of their iniquities" (Psalms 107:17 NIV)

Wade paced his apartment, waiting for the explosion. Any minute now, they will see who's in charge. He turned on the television, flip…nothing…flip…nothing…flip…nothing! Maybe he missed a call, so he checked his cellphone. Thumb up…nothing…Thumb down… nothing!

"What is going on? It has been hours. It should have aired by now!!!" The loud voices started laughing – louder! Pounding his head with the palm of his hand, "shut up! **Shut Up! SHUT UP!** I don't have time for you right now! I have to figure this out! I have to figure out why it isn't all over the news."

Breaking News Headlines…

"NAVY DECORATED LOCAL BUSINESS OWNER IMPRISONED"

"What happened?"

KNOCK…KNOCK…KNOCK…

On the other side of that knock was Wade's answer.

Wade was arrested for allegedly sending false accusations to the newspaper, falsifying government contract documents and forgery. This time he went to jail for himself. This time there was no one to frame.

…

The Evil One laughed, "You always thought you were smarter than the average criminal."

"I'm no criminal! Just **shut up!**"

The Voices continued, "Gregory tried to tell you, but you were too smart to listen – now look at you, trying to sabotage innocent people and here you are, about to be exposed, naked to the world!"

"Shut up!" yelled Wade, **"Just Shut up!"**

Wade implicated Joseph McIntosh and Christopher Gregory. Both squealed like little piglets and testified against Wade. Wade begged Antonio to bail him out. When Antonio didn't, Wade cursed him. He called him all kinds of horrible names that can't be repeated.

When he was arrested, he was unable to take his medication. Because Wade chose to hide his illness from everyone, his family did not know he was taking medication for a mental illness. By the time his doctor found out Wade had been arrested, he had already experienced several psychotic episodes. Wade's family was very upset to find out that for years, not only had he been diagnosed with schizophrenia and bipolar disorder, but he refused to tell them or allow his doctor to disclose any information. However, it explained many bizarre behaviors he explained away, as well as, his overdosing twice because he was using both legal and illegal drugs.

...

Although Wade was receiving his medication again, while in court, the voices were loud, causing him, on several occasions, to speak out of turn. Antonio asked the bailiff's permission for he or one of his sisters to sit closer to Wade, hoping that might calm him down. It did.

Wade was found guilty and sentenced to a three-year jail term. The first year of his term was counted as time served while awaiting trial and during the trial. Because he was diagnosed with the mental illnesses, the court ordered him to serve the remaining two-year sentence in the psychiatric hospital of the prison. He could have been sentenced for a longer term. However, under the circumstances, the court chose to be lenient. He received unprecedented grace. Despite his arrogance toward God, God allowed the South Carolina Justice System to show him grace. It was sad. He was in his mid-fifties and if he didn't pull himself together while incarcerated, he could die before he was released.

Fortunately for Wade, Chris Gregory could not take him to court to recoup his money and risk going to jail again for drug trafficking, and Joseph McIntosh lost any chance of acquiring MMTrucking.

All was well with the world for MMTrucking, but not for Antonio. He was heartbroken. His brother had gone to such lengths to destroy him for something that happened

...

before he was born. He worried about what would happen to his brother in prison. He wondered if he would ever find peace with himself and with God. He decided he would visit him as often as possible, even if Wade didn't want to see him. Maybe he might be able to find a clear spot in his spirit that will hear him and hear God. One of the psychiatrists in the hospital was a member of Lizanne's church. He visited Wade whenever he could.

Wade had completely shut down. He tried blaming God, even though he knew he really could no longer do that. Although he knew he was the reason he was in this predicament, he chose to remain angry. The on-staff psychiatrists could not help Wade as their caseloads were not conducive to an inmate needing constant help. As a result, Wade's illness became worst and The Voices became stronger.

Wade kept to himself in the hospital. He did not associate with anyone he didn't have to, refusing to participate in any programs not required. Antonio visited him every week, sometimes Wade would see him, sometimes he wouldn't. One visit was very traumatic. The Voices were very loud while Antonio tried to talk to him about making changes and reading the Bible. Wade yelled, cursed him, told him he never liked him and called him a half-and-half. Antonio sat there, allowing him to rant at him for a few minutes. Then he left.

Chapter 1
Dr. Tiffany Parker-Stewart

Dr. Tiffany Parker-Stewart is well known in her field of Brain and Cognitive Science, especially pertaining to her studies on the incarceration of inmates previously diagnosed with mental disorders. Dr. Parker-Stewart is currently in private practice as a Christian Psychiatrist and serves as the South Carolina State Prison Director of Mental Health Services.

Tiffany, like many other mental health professionals, became a therapist as a result of her own experiences and the obstacles she faced throughout her life. The trauma she endured and conquered led her to discover the professional path God intended for her.

Tiffany was raised in the "family" church where she enjoyed Pathfinders, the Youth Choir, Youth Club and many other programs her church offered. She especially enjoyed helping the nurses in the church clinic and assisted the health leader with various events. At the age of sixteen, she had an opportunity to attend a camp designed for teenagers considering a career in the medical field. She was in medical heaven. She even learned how to set broken bones. The camp sealed her desire to be a surgeon. That same year, Tiffany had an opportunity to help a doctor set someone's broken leg

...

while waiting for the ambulance to arrive. The doctor was so impressed with her skill, he gave her his contact information and promised to be available if she needed him during college and medical school. Eventually, he became her mentor, helping and supporting her through some tough times and decisions during her studies.

Her parents could not have been prouder of her. They did, however, have a very serious concern. They prided themselves upon the fact that all of their children were afforded a continuous Christian education, *all the way through college.* Tiffany chose to attend a secular university, instead of the one her parents and her siblings graduated from. Their college is one of the highest-rated Historically Black Colleges and Universities (HBCU) in academic and religious studies. The atmosphere of the college afforded students a continuing Christian lifestyle, adhering to the doctrines of their faith.

This was her parents and her siblings Alma Mata and, yes, they met their spouses on campus. It was assumed Tiffany would follow suit; however, her parents soon realized the anguish of having a "determined" youngest child headed to the college of *her* choice…not theirs.

Tiffany chose a secular university as it offered the program of study she wanted and more importantly, accepted her with a full scholarship, tuition, books and dormitory. Her parent's university did not offer her a scholarship comparable

...

to the scholarships offered from other universities. Tiffany's university had a highly accredited pre-med program. Although her parent's alma mater had an outstanding academic reputation, their medical program consisted of a variety of degree programs, such as nursing and physical therapy; however, there was no pre-med program. Her mother tried to entice her to become a nurse and join the university's world-renowned choir and music department. After all, she might become a pastor's wife, and everyone knows that pastor's wives sing and play the piano. Tiffany laughed so hard she couldn't breathe because her mother knew she couldn't hold a tune if they tied it around her waist; and a pastor for a husband was not even her last choice…in other words, not a consideration at all.

Her mother received her degree in education and became an excellent teacher and administrator in the Christian school system. However, she was most proud of her certificate of marriage to a theologian. Her father grew to be an awesome preacher, pastor and evangelist. However, he was proudest of his wife, as she was both a songstress and pianist, able to perform when and wherever he preached.

Unfortunately, Tiffany was the only of her sisters that did not *rise to the occasion* of a continued Christian education and with the honored certification as a pastor's wife. Needless to say, her parent's feelings were a little hurt from the idea of her not attending their Alma Mater.

When reality set in, her parents had to agree to the university of her choice and the career of her choice went hand-in-hand.

A secret reason she wanted to attend a secular university is because she was a very talented artist and she loved watching modern dance and ballet. The high school she attended taught art, but not ballet, as it was not in sync with their religion's doctrinal beliefs. At her chosen university, she will be able to pursue both as time permitted.

Amazingly, as artistic as she was, Tiffany's true love in junior high and high school was chemistry and biology, which is why she chose the medical field as her career choice. In college, she excelled in her pre-med classes, especially neurology. In her sophomore year, she was introduced to neuropsychology. She knew that was the field God purposed her for. The opportunity to help people understand the correlation between their physical/biological state and their mental state, and how to overcome mental obstacles preventing them from living a normal, prosperous and happy life enticed her. She still wanted to continue her study in medicine, although surgery was no longer her goal. She knew deep in her spirit that she was destined to help people escape the darkness that trapped them in their minds. So, upon

...

entering into her junior year of undergraduate studies, she continued her major in pre-med and added a second major in psychology. She chose not to tell her parents. She learned early on that her parents did not have a passion for the things they did not understand or agree with, which, most of the time, were things she was passionate about. The conversation always, always, always ended negatively. So, as a teenager, Tiffany became a professional secret keeper, not only her friend's secrets, but her own as well.

She spoke to her advisor about continuing her medical education in the field of Psychiatry with an emphasis in Neuropathology. She knew her parent's views, which is why she kept her innermost secrets from her parents. She had ample experience to know they would attempt to circumvent her plans for her future to coincide with their idea of what her future should look like.

Not only did she not seek their advice concerning her career change, she did not tell them about other adventures in her life, such as meeting and falling in love with a sailor. Her parents had nothing against military men as a group, since they had the sole responsibility of securing the safety of Americans from enemies, foreign and domestic. They probably would tolerate Tiffany's friend because he completed medical school and is currently an intern at a local hospital. The problem is he is not associated with their

...

religious denomination or any other *traditional* religious organization…basically…not a Christian, which in her parent's circle meant he was probably a heathen.

While home on a short break, she revealed her plans to her parents. Needless to say, her parent's initial reaction was shock, which then turned to anger. Tiffany was not surprised at their reaction to her boyfriend; however, she could not believe their negative, illogical, backwards thinking reaction to her career change. They believed the study of psychology was related to spiritualism and Satan worshipping, which, they felt, explained her lowered zeal for her Christian religion.

She knew this conversation was taking a turn for the worse, when they obviously forgot she was an adult and said they should have never *allowed* her to go to a secular college where she was influenced by the lack of biblical teachings, friends and professors. Second, they declared her "heathen" boyfriend to be the reason for her obvious loss of thought and spiritual upbringing. Tiffany, in a desperate attempt to protect her ability to make the decisions about her life, told her parents her spiritual life was as strong as she needed it to be. They were not listening. They felt her choice of college and boyfriend interfered with her Sabbath hours, her church attendance, her choice to wear make-up and jewelry and now making the decision to change her major without discussing it with them first.

Tiffany smiled when she remembered how upset they were when she reminded them their alma mater offered psychology as a major field of study. Her mother looked at her as if she was considering backhanding her right in the mouth!

Tiffany couldn't believe how unreasonable her parents were over her decision, although not a small decision, nevertheless, still her decision, not theirs.

Even though she was 20 years old and capable of making her own adult decisions, Tiffany's parents felt they had the authority to demand she change her mind about studying psychiatry and get rid of her boyfriend.

Once her mother came to the realization they would not be able to persuade her to change her mind, they did what most Christian parents do. They solicited the help of their pastor to mediate an intervention. However, the intervention did not turn out the way they planned.

Because Tiffany loved her parents and she knew they were just trying to help her make good decisions, she agreed to a family meeting to discuss her future. Tiffany expected to see her parents and her siblings. When their Pastor walked in, she was immediately angry and refused to respond to anything he asked or said. She treated him the same way Jesus

...

treated Herod. She refused to answer any of his questions. When her father insisted she responded, as politely as she could, Tiffany told her father she was told this would be a family meeting and "your" pastor is not family. Therefore, she had nothing to discuss *with him*. Her father was about to respond when his wife gently placed her hand on his knee. This was their signal to each other to tone it down. As it is with dads, he could not understand what was wrong with his daughter. However, her mother sensed something wasn't being spoken…something Tiffany and this pastor knew, something that had not been voiced to others. She had heard rumors of the pastor acting inappropriately towards some of the young ladies. In the back of her mind, she remembered Tiffany mentioned something about this pastor's inappropriate behavior and dismissed it. She wondered if she made a mistake. She remembered saying to her daughter, "He's the Pastor. I don't understand why anyone would start such a horrible rumor about a pastor, especially my daughter." But now…she wondered?

Tiffany was sad that her parents could not see she was happy with her choices; however, she understood them. In their world, remaining separate from the secular way of doing things, holding on to old beliefs and traditions of their faith was imperative for a full spiritual life. They believed unequally yoked only referred to never marrying a member of another religious organization. They believed psychology, by itself, was harmless; however, the techniques of many mental health providers was not Biblical; and some, such as hypnosis, resemble voodoo and spiritualism. It didn't help matters that they recently watched a documentary about mental health professionals and their idea of divine verses scientific intervention when working with their clients. It also did not help that the research revealed, even though about 60 percent of mental health professionals were Christians, only about 40 percent of the Christian therapists believed a divine power was responsible for their ability to diagnose and treat clients.

Tiffany's parents tried to encourage her to continue counseling sessions with the pastor, in hopes she would "come to her senses." Again, Tiffany tried to make her parents understand she had no intention of changing her major and absolutely no desire to speak to their pastor, in person, nor by phone. Finally, she told them she would not speak to him, even if it meant disrespecting their wishes.

When they met with the pastor to let him know Tiffany's decision, they were surprised how he became visibly angry and insisted on private sessions with her in person. If she declined, he would recommend the church censor her until she agreed to meet with him. Now her father had questions. He knew there were no grounds for the church to censor his daughter, so he was curious as to why the pastor

...

would make such an idle threat, knowing he didn't have this authority and the church would not approve it. Of course, Tiffany declined the pastor's preference, and to her surprise, her parents agreed with her.

Chapter 2: Session 3
Anger Works!

Dr. Stewart's notes: Today I am meeting with my newest client, Wade. He is diagnosed with schizophrenia and bipolar disorder. This is our third session and now that we have completed the niceties of our greetings, it's time we get down to business ...

"Wade, I've been reading over the personal history form you filled out for me last week. I noticed you mentioned being angry 'all your life' several times. Please explain to me what this anger is and how does it make you feel?"

Wade sat in the chair, with his head in his hands, as if he had a headache...

"Didn't you see on that paper I was a Halloween baby? Yes. There are only a few times I can remember not being angry. Like when I was eleven years old, and I went to Puerto Rico to be the "best man" in my dad's wedding to Marguerite, his new wife. In the few days, we were in Puerto Rico, I felt more love there from my new Abuelos and Abuelita, aunts, uncles and cousins than I had ever had in my entire life. The only other people who showed me such love were Grammee and Papa, my dad's parents. They loved me and treated me like they loved me. Even though we all lived in the same town, once my parents divorced, it became more and more difficult for me to spend time with them. Once in a while, my mom would take me to visit with them. Otherwise, I was only able to spend time with them whenever Papa was able to come for me or whenever my dad was in town."

"I remember anger when my mom remarried, and her new husband moved us far away from Grammee and Papa and my mother's parents. Afterwards, the only time I saw them was when my dad was in town, He would pick me up and we would stay in Beaufort for the weekend. I really wanted to live with Grammee and Papa until I could go live with my dad, but it wasn't allowed. When my mother married the man she married, I couldn't do anything, especially anything involving the Martin family. He was a hateful…(um)…well…(hum)…I'm trying not to say what my brain wants to call him…he was just hateful, and I hated him."

The look on Wade's face was very concerning, as though even the memory brought him unbearable pain.

"My mother's parents were a strange breed of people. My grandfather was one of those 'proud – black - Baptist deacon - holier-than-thou – hypocrites."

There was a look of total disdain on Wade's face as he described his grandfather, as if he would throw-up any second.

"My grandmother followed him around as she was taught – without question."

"What do you mean "as she was taught?"

"When I was older, my grandmother told me her mother taught her the wife was to be totally obedient and submissive to her husband. Before she died, I asked her why they forced my mom and me to live with that hateful man. She said her parents married her to my grandfather and she "stuck it out." She said my grandfather thought my stepfather was the best husband for my mom. Before I knew the words were coming out of my mouth, I told her my real dad was the best husband for her…then I had to apologize because, despite everything, in some ways, she was a victim just like me and my mom. At that moment, I felt more sorry for her than I did for myself. From then on, I tried to love her better. It was easier when my grandfather was not around…and when I say, "not around"…I mean…DEAD!"

"My grandparents never seemed to have a logical explanation as to why they thought they had the right to destroy my parent's marriage and then marry her off to who *they* wanted her to be married to, who *they* thought would be best for her and a better father for me. What God gave them the authority to split up my mom from a man that was a good husband who loved her and wanted to be with us…and married her off to a monster! They looked at his position in church, his car, his money and thought that would make up for the fact that he was a horrible person. My grandfather

...

should have married him because they were two peas in a pod. Self-righteous and full of… *sigh* …themselves.

"But," *he stopped talking as another dark wave shadowed his face,* "I wonder…" *he turned to look at me with a solemn look in his eyes,* "I wonder if my grandfather knew…*everything*. The Voices always told me he didn't care."

I knew this would be an answer controlled by anger, but I asked him, "Why do you think your grandfather was hateful and a hypocrite?"

"As the story goes, my mother and father met in high school, fell in teenage love and teenage parenthood. My mom told me a couple of days after she told her parents she was pregnant, she overheard her father discussing abortion, but her mother, for the first time, shut him down. I never told my mom The Voices said my grandmother should have let him kill me then."

Again, he paused. This time he stood up and walked over to the window, rubbing his eyes, face and bald head, as if he was trying to rub the memories out of his thoughts.

He then turned to me and said, "You know, I don't ever remember my grandmother standing up for me or my mom, except one time. Despite everything, I am glad she did that day."

"In your personal history, you wrote how you hate your brother. Once you even said you hate him, but you love him…"

...

"I don't think I really started being angry until my half-brother, Antonio, was born. Until then, I had my dad's full attention. He was born with a twin sister, Maria. I like her, I guess because she did not really pose a threat when it can to the affections of my real dad."

Antonio, on the other hand, got on my nerves from the moment he took his first breath."

Just as I was about to ask him why, he looked at me, shook his head and said…

'Don't ask me why. I don't know why. He was always a good kid, annoying and no matter how horrible I treated him, he loved me. I knew he loved me. His mother, Marguerite, was a Spaniard, so I would call him "half and half," when he really got on my nerves and when I thought no one was listening. You want to know why I hated and loved him, because, no matter what I did, he seemed to always be there for me…like now. He knew I was being an a…well, you know…not nice, but he would smile, and love me anyway."

He seems to be remembering and talking at the same time. As if he could hear him and Antonio in an unpleasant conversation.

"I was twelve when the twins were born. Have you seen the first series of the movie 'The Mummy'? Remember the sandstorm with the mummy's mouth…anyways, I always felt I was fighting my way out of a sandstorm, trying to get

...

away from the demons and closer to my dad. I knew it wasn't my fault and it was not always my dad's fault. I knew my grandfather and stepfather went out of their way to wreck my relationship with my dad and that my grandmother and mom were afraid of both of them. Regardless, I let myself believe Antonio was taking the little bit of love I was getting from my dad, with none left for me. After we were adults, I believed dad proved how much he didn't love me when he turned the entire business over to Antonio. It didn't matter to me if it was a repercussion of the things I did to sabotage the business and the family. I can't even blame it on The Voices. I always knew I could ignore them, if I really wanted too. Well, except for the Evil One. He was too strong. Looking back, I knew there was no way to exhaust my dad or Antonio's love, but I was stubborn, and The Loud Voices made sure I ignored all of their efforts.

Chapter 3: *Session 4*
At Least The Whisperers Care Enough…

"Wade, can you remember the first time you heard voices?"

Wade did not immediately answer. He sat in silence for a couple minutes. He did not want to talk about The Voices, and he did not want to remember anything. He looked at me to show he was not in the mood.

"Even though my mom's parents *pretended* to be good people, they were horrible parents and grandparents. As far as I am concerned, it is their fault, my life was so jacked up. It is their fault my mom suffered with that lunatic for so long. I am so glad she never had babies with him, almost…"

His voice trailed off as if he was remembering something horrible, something he never wanted to remember again. After a long silence, he sighed and continued…

"When I was ten, my mom was pregnant. When she was seven months pregnant, he beat her because he wanted her to do something she could not do. I was in my room studying for a math exam. I was accustomed to hearing them fight, even while she was pregnant. However, this was different. I heard her voice screaming and crying. Then, I didn't hear it anymore. When I heard something fall, I ran into the kitchen and saw her on the floor, him leaning over and choking her. I tried to pull him off of her, but he was too heavy. I was about to panic when I saw the bowl his mom

...

had given my mom. I grabbed it and smashed it over his head."

He raised both his hands over his head, as if he was holding something. and threw it to the floor and bent over as if he was looking at something on the floor. Then he looked at me, smiled and said...

"That was the ugliest bowl...and I'm sure it was happy to die." "When the bowl hit him, he fell over. Unfortunately, he was not dead...only the bowl."

"Fortunately for him, just as I was about to hit him again, our neighbor ran through the door. Good thing it wasn't locked because if she had not shown up right then, I would have killed him. I remember a loud, mean voice I had never heard before yelling, **"Kill him! Kill him! You and your mom will be better off!"** It scared me because I did not know where the voices came from. That was the first time I remember hearing voices other than The Whisperers. Between the voices yelling in my head and my neighbor yelling in my ears, I dropped whatever it was in my hand and kicked him several times."

"My mom was beaten badly and barely breathing by the time the ambulance arrived. The police locked him up. On the way to the hospital, my mom went into labor. The baby was born. It was a girl. She was dead. I could have had another little sister if it were not for that ba...hmmm...that man. Do you know what the worst part of this whole

...

nightmare was? He just had a couple of cuts, a broken rib and some bruises. Other than that, he wasn't hurt. My mother almost died…and my sister did die! My mom pressed charges. He was charged with assaulting my mother. Because the baby died as a direct result of the assault, he was charged with murdering the baby. His defense lawyer tried to prove the baby was a fetus and not a person and therefore, he could not be charged with murder. Fortunately, that lie didn't fly over too well with the jury nor with the judge. He was sentenced to twelve years, two for beating my mom and ten for killing my sister. My mother's life was only worth TWO YEARS and TEN YEARS is the cost of a life that never got a chance to live…only ten years. Disgusting…"

"At that moment, I did not know who I hated more, him or my grandfather. I **HATED** him for so many years I stopped counting. And I hated my grandparents for allowing him to treat us the way he did. They did not believe me or my mom until he almost killed her, and I almost killed him. I was angry with my dad and his parents for not taking me away from everything; but, if they had, my mom would be dead. So I don't hate them. The Whisperers told me not to hate anyone. I tried not to hate my grandfather, but it was impossible to love him. He made sure of that."

"*Wade, so as far as you can remember, the first time you heard voices was at this point when your stepfather was hurting your mother.*"

...

"No, I just didn't know what it was or where it was coming from. I did not hear the mean voices before that night and not again for many years. Until after high school, I did not hear voices often, however, whenever I did, they were quiet and soothing... *The Whisperers.* That's what I use to call them."

"That's an interesting name for them, 'The Whisperers.'"

"I called them that because for a long time I would have nightmares about the night when he tried to kill my mother and about other bad things and The Whisperers would talk softly to me and tell me everything was gonna be alright."

Have you heard The Whisperers or other pleasant voices since you have become an adult?

"Once or twice, mostly when I was sad or having an anxiety attack. Sometimes, if it was really bad, Abuelita would talk to me."

"He's dead now... finally."

"Who is dead now?"

"My stepfather, and not soon enough. Remember, I told you they decided the life of my mom and sister was only worth twelve years?"

"Yes"

"Well, they poured even more salt in our wounds."

He paused and was silent for a moment.

...

"Wade, how did they pour salt in the wounds of your mother and you?"

"He did not serve the entire twelve years, only eight. Good behavior. There was nothing good about him. I guess there was no one in prison he could beat up on, so he stayed out of trouble. Even worse than getting out of prison early was him begging my mom to let him move back in with her because he was sick, and he had no one to care for him. After the horrible way he treated my mom and me, he wanted her to take care of him like he deserved to be taken care of. I was so relieved when she immediately told him no. I think she was afraid I would have killed him the first chance I got! And she was right! Stab him right through the heart like the vampire leech he was!"

"Why would he come to your mother?"

"They were still married. At first, she wanted to divorce him, but for some reason, she changed her mind about the divorce. Being a Christian and all, I guess she felt obligated to help him get into a nursing home. He had severe high blood pressure and had two strokes while he was in prison, which caused other medical problems. All of this eventually caused damaged kidneys. With the deterioration of his health, he was not eligible for a kidney transplant, so, he was on dialysis for the rest of his life.

...

I'm sure that's why they let him out early. They called it "good behavior." I expect they did not want him to die in prison. The prison had been having bad press because the number of medical deaths was very high. They were just trying to avoid more bad publicity... that's just my opinion."

"Anyways, my mom went to see him often in the nursing home just to make sure he was being cared for properly. Doc, I don't care much for God these days and I'm sure he could care less about me. However, He had better make sure my momma gets everything she wants in heaven, because she is a saint down here; and that's all I have to say about that!!!"

"I will tell you what really p...!"

He again stood up and walked towards the window.

"I'm sorry, Doc, my tongue almost got away from me. What really made me mad was him showing up at my high school graduation! Ruined my entire day. I did not want him anywhere near me, and especially not on my graduation day. I don't know how he got a ticket. I'm sure my mom gave it to him. My whole family was there. My mom and grandmother, my dad, his family and Grammee and Papa. I did not even want my grandfather there, but I knew my mom would have been upset with me if I had not invited him, especially since he was ill and in a wheelchair. My whole family had never been in the same room, as far as I can

...

remember. My dad shook their hands and introduced them to his family. I, on the other hand, tried to avoid touching my grandfather at all. I could hear a loud voice trying to talk me into making a scene. The Whisperers told me to remember what it took for me to get to that moment, with honors, so I did not act out."

"When my grandmother came to hug me, she had tears in her eyes. I was happy to hug her back, because driving her around gave me a chance to really get to know her. I learned she was a prisoner in her own home. She told me she loved me and was very proud of me. I told her I love her too. My mom's husband stayed away from me and I stayed away from him. A few weeks later, he was in the obituaries."

"After graduation, we went out to dinner. My dad had made all of the arrangements. Everyone, except my grandfather, talked about how proud they were of me, graduating, with honors, followed by the 'you-have-your-whole-life-ahead-of-you' speech. That was one of the very few times I can say I felt much love from, and for, my family."

"Then, my mom's father decided he had to say something. He couldn't stand the thought of everyone complimenting me and showing love for me...the mistake born on Halloween. Because he was very sick and had to use

...

oxygen tubes, his voice was gruff and raspy. When he talked, it seemed as if he had no more air left after a couple words, and he sounded like he swallowed a brillo pad. It was pitiful. As much as I hated him, I was sad he had dwindled to almost nothing.

He asked me which college I had chosen. When I told him MMTrucking Drivers College and Technical School in Beaufort, he tried to yell, *"That's not a real (gasp) college!" Despite everything (cough-gasp-cough), your grades were (gasp) such that you could go to any (cough-gasp-cough) real four-year university(cough-cough-gasp-cough)."*

"At this point, my grandmother tried to calm and quiet him down. He continued with his rant, and cough, and gasp for air, and cough some more, just a little quieter, "It's bad enough *(gasp-cough)* you refused to go *(gasp)* to my alma mater *(cough-gasp-cough)* after I made the necessary *(gasp)* calls to get you admitted. *(cough-gasp-cough-gasp)*

"I'd kill myself first before I attended that school!"

Wade saw the shocked look on Dr. Stewart's face...

Wade laughed, "Well, I didn't say it out loud, but I wanted to!"

Grandfather continues, "Now you are *(cough-gasp)* not going to a university *(gasp)* at all... but to some trucking school *(gasp-cough-cough-cough)*. I'm sure he coerced *(gasp)* you into giving up *(gasp-cough)* great opportunities, to do what!,

...

(cough-gasp-cough-gasp) drive trucks! *(cough-cough-gasp)* I guess next you'll *(cough-cough-gasp)* be joining the Navy!" *(cough-cough-gasp-cough-gasp)*

Just as I was about to respond, The Whisperers said, "Let your father handle this…".

"Then my father, Senior Chief Marcus Anthony Martin, United States Navy, Retired – President and Chief Executive Officer of MMTrucking, INC, stood up and faced my grandfather."

As if Wade wanted to make sure I could see the scene, he stood up and squared his shoulders the way a military person would do.

"It seemed as if he was standing twelve feet over my grandfather. I remember his words as if it were yesterday."

"You, sir, have been a disrespectful man and a tyrant for as long as I have known you. However, this is where it stops. My son will attend any school he chooses to attend, in Beaufort, or anywhere else. It is his choice. He will learn to drive trucks and how to manage the business, because, that's what he wants to do. No one coerced him. This is the career choice he has made, at least for now. You, sir, have no say in this matter."

Grandfather opened his mouth to say something, but dad raised his hands, like this…*(Wade held up his hand, palm facing me as to say '**STOP**')* and said, "Good night," and the Martins left the table, including me.

I felt bad for my grandmother and my mom – they were both in tears. It had been such a wonderful day, and he had to ruin it for everyone. That's what he did…ruined life for everyone.

"A miserable heart means a miserable life…"
Proverbs 15:15a (MSG)

Chapter 4: Session 7
What's Love Got To Do With It...

"Hello, Wade, so how have you been since our last meeting?"

With much sarcasm, "Well, you know Doc, I spent the last couple days at Trivoli Gardens in Copenhagen. Did you know they have a wicked amusement park!" *Wade was rolling his eyes, pouting and even sneered as he spoke.* "How do you think my days have been, considering I'm still living in this hospital that looks and feels and smells a whole lot like prison!"

"Hmmm...Did something happen? Why are you so agitated?"

"I really don't want to talk about it, but I know you will aggravate me until I tell you something...truth or not, it don't matter...as long as I tell you something, so you stop bugging me about it!"

"I would hope you tell me the truth and allow me to help if I can."

"Sure..." *He sighed as if it may be his last breath...as if something was weighing very heavy on his heart. He was silent for a moment...*

"I'm sure you know somebody died in here last night. They said it was 'natural causes.' *Wade held up his fingers in the quotation symbol and smirked.* "They said he had a heart attack, but it wasn't."

"How do you know it wasn't?"

...

"One of the voices told me—the quiet one. Sometimes I hear her fussing at the others when they are out of control. I was surprised they understood her. It's my abuelita's voice, Marguerite's mom. She doesn't speak English. I learned Spanish because of Marguerite, my Abuelos and family. Abuelita always spoke to me in Spanish and now the voice I hear is her soft voice speaking to me in Spanish." She said, *"Nieto tenga mucho cuidado porque los guardias y los camilleros son malos. Lastimen a las personas que no pueden defenderse y salir con la suya... son muy malos".*

"In English, she was warning me to be very careful because the guards and orderlies are bad. They hurt people that can't fight back and get away with it…they are very bad."

"I agree with her, because I've seen them beat people when they couldn't do whatever…"

He turned to me with a cold stare…

"If anyone of them touches me wrong…it's all over…I just want you to know…I **will** be in here forever, for murder."

I knew he was serious, so there was nothing else to say.

"One of the orderlies had music on and that song "What's Love Got To Do With It" was playing. You know Tina Turner…You do know who Tina Turner is, don't you, Doc?"

Now it was Dr. Stewart's turn to roll her eye…

...

42

"Yes, Wade, I know who Tina Turner is…dah!"

"I just wanted to make sure, because some of y'all act as if you don't live in the same world your clients live in!"

I had to laugh because he's right. Some of my colleagues are quite hob snobbish.

"Well, the song made me remember how my grandmother and her sisters used to say that about my parents. She would say love had nothing to do with good breeding. Even though she didn't call my name, I knew she was talking about me."

He shook his head…

"I am so glad my grandmother and I became friends. For many years I thought she was as bad as my grandfather. However, when he got sick, she became more independent. One day, when I was a teenager, she took me and my mom out to dinner and apologized for everything she had done and allowed my grandfather to do. She told us she was afraid of my grandfather and she taught my mom to be afraid of him. I wanted to scream at her because of the hell my mom and I had been through, but I didn't because my mom was crying, and I didn't want to make it worse. Over time, she told me much of what I'm telling you. I'm glad we became friends before she died."

"When did she die?"

"A couple of years back, before all of this happened. It would have broken her heart to see me here."

"I told her about The Voices a few months before she died. I knew she believed me this time. She told me my grandfather had schizophrenia. She wanted me to tell my dad and mom, but I didn't. She said she didn't know much about it; however, she was sure my issues are a result of how he treated me. She cried. I wished I had not told her. So I lied and told her I was fine with it. I told her I was taking my medication and was living a great life and I would be alright."

"My parents stayed married for two or three years before they got divorced. I don't even remember them being married. I think I must have decided that day I would NEVER love anyone, get married and I will definitely NEVER...EVER... have children."

I asked the question, feeling I already knew the answer...

"Why didn't you ever marry or want children?"

"For what reason. I never had a good childhood. How could I help a kid have a good childhood or a good life?"

Chapter 5: *Session 8*
What's In A Name

Wade was in an uncommonly grouchy mood when he came into my office. He said The Voices almost got him into a fight and it was hard shutting them up. I reminded him he was the grown-up, not the voices. He said sometimes they were clearly the grown-ups, and that he did not want to talk about his grandfather…but he did.

"My grandfather had no clue what he was doing when he bullied his name on me. My grandfather wanted to stick it to my dad and show him he was in control of everyone's life, including my dad's and mine. When I came out a boy, out of pure hatred, he tricked my mother into naming me after him, instead of after my dad. My dad was at sea, so he could not be there when I was born. It made it easier for my grandfather to make sure I was named what he wanted, instead of what she wanted."

"How did he 'trick' your mother into doing that…"

"My grandfather intercepted the birth certificate application and filled it out. My mother and grandmother were afraid of my grandfather, so they pretty much did whatever he wanted them to do. Like I said, he was mean and arrogant and a bully."

"How was your grandfather able to control what you would be named? Your mother or father had to write the name on the paperwork."

...

"My grandmother told me after he died, he forged the paperwork; this *man of God* forging government documents. People are always asking me why I don't care much for God. What type of God would allow him to be in charge of his church knowing he's a thief and a liar?"

"Why didn't your mother redo the paperwork once she discovered the forgery?"

"I'm sure she did not want to be the cause of her father going to prison for forging government documents. As far as I'm concerned, we would have all been better off!"

"Needless to say, you have survived, even with your grandfather's name..."

Wade interrupted...

"Doc, you know as well as I, a person's name, whether it's a good name or a bad name, is the beginning of a person's identity. That's why people are always changing their names. I should have changed my name, but I didn't. We had become accustomed to it, even though I was named after the Devil himself. Yep, *(he sort of snickered)* the Devil has a name and it is Timothy Wade..."

"The only blessing in the whole ordeal was he could not change my last name, because my mom's last name was Martin, my father's name. Also, my mom refused to call me Timothy. She called me Wade and she put Wade on my school records so everyone, except my grandfather, would

...

call me Wade. My grandfather called me Timothy to be spiteful. I guess it made him feel good about himself. He would introduce me to his friends as Timothy and pound on his chest about how great it was his grandson was named after him. My grandmother or my mom would always correct him and tell them to call me Wade. He would be furious," *Wade snickered as he continued,* "When I was old enough, I asked him not to call me Timothy, because my name was Wade."

"YOU WERE NAMED AFTER ME!!!" He would yell.

"Yes, grandfather, my government name is Timothy Wade Martin. **However**, the name I go by is Wade."

"I had a few defiant moments in my life, so whenever possible, I did not respond when he called me Timothy."

"I had to be careful because he was an abusive bully…he used to beat me. He hated my father and he hated me from the moment I was born. I never understood why he wanted someone he hated so much to carry his name or why he didn't just let me live with my father?

"I really believe my grandfather and my step-father are the reason The Voices came."

"I can honestly say for most of my life, my life mirrored my names. I see now why I was diagnosed with Schizophrenia and Bipolar Disorder. Doc, I bet in all of your years in this work of helping crazy people like me, you have

...

never come across anything so conflicting, so opposing, as my name."

Timothy: *Honored by God*

Wade: *Resisting movement*

Martin: *Warlike / A Warrior*

Wade walked across the room and stood in front of the window, which had become his way when he was frustrated.
"How can a man be honored by God while he is a resistant warrior? What is that all about! Doc, can you explain it? No, you can't!… Nobody can! My grandfather's plan to spit in my father's face splattered all over mine. If taking my father's name from me was the worst thing he had ever done, I would have had a wonderful relationship with my grandfather; but it was nothing compared to the horrible life he doled out to my mother and me. He was Satan and he proved it every day of his life. And I was named after Satan, and I proved that every day of my life. Why do you think God hates me? Why do you think The Voices live in me every moment of my life?"

"You do know that's why we are here, talking to you, don't you?!"

Chapter 6: *Session 10*
Marcus Meets Phyllis

"Good morning. How have you been since our last…"

Dr. Stewart cut her words short because something caught her attention…

"Why do you have hair?"

Wade laughed. "My barber is in solitary confinement for threatening to cut someone and I was not about to let the 'Sweet Boys' touch my head!"

Wade laughed and sat back on the couch.

"You keep asking me about my parents. I guess you are trying to figure out how much of my damage is their fault! Isn't that what you do, blame it on the mothers!"

Rolling his eyes, he continued, "Anyways, I told you before I did a lot of eavesdropping when I was a child. Otherwise, I would have been as dumb as a rock about my family history."

"My mother is an only child, living the life of an only child whose parents were affluent in the community and the church. Her mother was a debutant and a Delta…I'm sure you know what Delta means…"

"Delta Sigma Theta Sorority, Incorporated. Yes, I know who they are."

"Are you one?"

"No."

"My grandmother was one, as was her mother and her mother before her. She expected my mom to do the same. Her mother was a nurse and Phyllis, that's my mom's name...Phyllis. Anyways, it was expected Phyllis would become a nurse too."

Wade chuckled as he continued, "It didn't matter to them that my mom fainted then, and still faints, at the sight of a needle or blood. Scraped knees in our house was a major catastrophe! My mom wanted to study art and music. She wanted to be a teacher. She was good at art and music. That's how she met my dad, in a school concert. My mom was in the school choir and played the piano. My dad, his name was Marcus, played the saxophone. Me too...I play the saxophone."

"I'm sorry, say what now? Did I understand you correctly? Did you say you play the saxophone?"

"Yes," *again chuckling,* "you seem surprised...sometimes I give those voices something constructive to do like sing when I play! Hahahaha!"

"My mom sang on the youth choir at her church. She was also the pianist. My dad told me his church would not allow him to play his saxophone very often. They were very conservative, and saxophones did not belong in the church. So he played at his friend's church and in the school band.

...

My dad used to tell me God will always provide an opportunity to do anything we are doing for Him. As I got older, I decided God could care less what I could or couldn't do."

"My grandfather complained about my saxophone playing, not because I was bad, because I wasn't bad...I, was VERY GOOD. He didn't like it because my mom said it reminded her of my dad's playing. I played once or twice at church because my mom asked me to. I played "Falling In Love With Jesus and We Fall Down" with her youth choir. It was fun. After I stopped going to church, I played in a little street corner band me and some of my friends created."

Wade had a faraway look in his eyes, shook his head slowly and pretty much talking to himself he said, "I haven't spoken to those guys in many, many years. When The Voices got too hard to handle, I stopped playing with the group. I didn't tell them, or anyone else, about the voices. I tried to tell my mom, but she had her own issues dealing with that lunatic she married. My grandfather chalked it up to me being demon-possessed; either way, I didn't get any help, so I stopped talking about it."

Again Wade paused, rubbed his head as if he were smoothing down the waves in his hair. He did not talk for a minute or so. After a short moment, he looked at me...and then with a sigh...

"Back to my parents. They both graduated from high school before I came along. They were in their first classes in

...

the local junior college, that's what they used to call technical colleges. He was in the truck driving certification program. In this class, he was able to receive a CDL Class B license. He could drive small trucks, but he could not drive the "big rigs." He wanted to continue training for his class A certification so he could get a job and be on the road. Thanks to the Vietnam War draft, he could not complete the certification. At least with his B class license, he was able to get a local job until he was drafted."

"From what little my parents told me and from overhearing grown folk conversations, I figured out other than band practice and performances, their paths did not cross, but somehow, by the spring semester in high school, they were in a whirlwind 'secret non-romance-romance-thingy' according to my mom's version of the story. Although he liked her a lot, my dad told me they were not high school sweethearts. He was from the wrong side of town. She was a debutant and her parents would have had a cow if they found out she was hanging out with the "likes of him." So they hung out whenever they could, mainly at games and other events at school. Somehow, they ended up having 'awkward sex' behind the bleachers on the football field. I overheard my grandmother and her sisters talking about it.

When I was old enough, I did ask my mom. She said she and my father were both virgins and 'it' was the most

...

horrible experience she had ever had and decided it was not worth repeating – EVER! Obviously, she changed her mind since I'm here talking to you! I'm sorry I'm jumping ahead. I have a headache today."

"They ran into each other again at the local recreation center at a sock hop."

"A what…I'm sorry a sock hop? What's a sock hop?"

With an almost disdained look on his face, he replied,

"A sock hop was a Saturday Night dance for teenagers. It was at the Recreation Center on the basketball floor, so everyone had to take off their shoes and dance in their socks!"

"Ah, hmmm…never heard of it, but I see how it makes sense and sounds fun."

"Anyways, they started seeing each other, again, on the sly. Again, awkward sex. Again horrible. My mom said sex was over-rated and not worth it, so she really started avoiding my dad because she didn't want sex anymore. By the end of the semester, she realized avoiding him was not gonna fix the problem.

"My mom told me she was terrified when she realized she was pregnant. They were both eighteen. She was in college, studying music and teaching. She was still taking general studies classes. She knew her parents would kill her, but she was more concerned about how my dad would react

...

to the news. They had only been going together for a short period of time and had only been together twice in over a year. How could she be pregnant! She had just started college and would have to drop out because, in 1956, unwed mothers were not allowed to go to school with the *good girls*. She was devastated. So, in order to finish out her first year of college, from February to May, she hid the pregnancy from everyone, even my dad. "

"By the end of the semester, she was no longer able to hide me. She could tell her mother suspected something. My dad said he was pretty shocked when she told him she was pregnant. He didn't really know what to say to her. She was crying so much he was afraid to say the wrong thing. He knew she didn't know everything about him, but he was hurt she thought he might walk out on her or suggest I belonged to someone else. He said the moment she told him he had every intent on doing the honorable thing. He said his dad taught him the choice is simple… 'wait or don't wait.' Wait meant keeping your hands, your mouth, your body parts and your mind to yourself. Choosing not to wait creates the possibility of a baby. If there's a baby… there needs to be a wife. I agreed, which is why I have no wife and no babies."

"My dad said he was not thinking about a baby nor a wife; however, my parents were raised during a time when pregnancy meant marriage. My dad had finished his training

...

and was working a little job, so as far as he was concerned, he was able to care for a wife and a baby."

"Although his parents were disappointed in his situation, they loved him still and vowed to support him and his family in any way they could. My mom's parents, however, were furious *she* had **gotten herself** pregnant. When she told her parents she and my dad were getting married, her parents were delirious with anger. Immediately her mother planned to send her on "vacation" to her Aunt Maggie's in Detroit. That's what was done when southern girls got pregnant. I guess northern girls were sent to their Aunt Maggie's in Mississippi *(he laughed)."*

"Well, the more she tried to explain he was joining the Navy and she would be well taken care of, the less they listened. So, my parents decided to get married immediately. They quickly married at the courthouse so we would have benefits and she could stay in college. He enlisted in the Navy the next week and left."

"Didn't their parents have to sign for them to get married? Okay, I'm being nosey, but I'm pretty sure in the 50s her parents would have had to give their permission."

Wade laughed, "I didn't ask, and she didn't say."

"So to continue with what I do know…once she was a married, pregnant woman, my mom was able to continue

...

school to finish her general studies classes so she would not get too far behind."

"Wade, when you heard these stories from your parents, how did it make you feel about them and about yourself?"

He paused as if deciding whether he would answer me or not…then laughing out loud, he continued…

"When I was about fifteen, my dad told me sex is like that old commercial, '…a little dab'll do ya…?' He was joking, but he was serious; he said I was old enough to hear and understand the truth. He wanted to make sure I understood the consequences of every action taken. He said they *attempted* sex twice – a year apart. That one time was all it took to bring me into the world. My grandfather always said I was an accident, a mistake. My dad said, although he and my mother should not have been 'dabbing' in grown folk activities, I was not an accident because God allowed me to be born for a reason. God wanted me to be born because He has plans for my life. I still laugh when I hear him in my head saying, *'Wade, you just have to hear Him tell you what His plan is.'*"

"What nonsense. When I was little, I believed him, but when 'The Voices' got loud, I stopped listening to my dad or believing in God. After he died, there was no one I would listen to, reminding me about God and me being wonderfully made, blah…blah…blah. However, there are times when I wish I had listened to my dad more, The Voices less, and started to believe in God again."

(Session Note: At that moment, Wade's expression was that of a boy, wishing for his father. He seems so sad. I want to get to the root of all of his sadness; however, I don't want to push him too quickly. He seems to be controlled by The Voices, so much so, I wonder how much of what he is telling me is his words and how much is their words. He tries to present this hard-shelled persona, but he seems so very fragile. I can't afford to crack that shell just yet. I need to soften it up just a little bit more.)

Chapter 7: *Session 13*
A Grandfather's Legacy

Legacy (leg-a-cy), a bequest, anything passed down from the past...

Wade's guard brought him to my office for an unscheduled visit and told me Wade had been in his cell for a couple days, muttering to himself and refuse to eat. Wade came into my office, spoke, and sat on the couch with his head in his hands, as if he had a headache, muttering to himself. Before I could ask, he said,

"Do you remember me telling you my grandfather knew all along about schizophrenia and voices. This is what I inherited from him. When my grandmother told me, she just cried. She told me she thought she was protecting him and everyone else by keeping it a secret. He is the reason I am like this. This is his legacy passed down to me."

Wade reached for the tissue box as he continued.

"My grandparents continuously reminded my mom that marrying my dad was a grave mistake and divorcing him at least salvaged some of her life. They would say his parents were not prominent in the Black community and my father was a street hoodlum who ruined her life by getting her pregnant with me. Once I overheard a conversation between my mom and her mother. *"He was not right for you,"* that's what *my grandmother said. "His family is not from our side of town. You were a debutante, destined to become a Delta. He ruined your life."*

...

"I remember hearing my mother fire back at her saying…"

"Marcus did not ruin my life; you and my father ruined my life and my son's life! You are my mother, you could have saved me from the hell me and Wade lived through with that demon, but you didn't. And I was too stupid and afraid to realize I did not have to listen to either one of you!"

They did not know I was listening, because it was grown folk talk. After hearing everything, I felt different about a few things."

"Soon enough, I realized my grandfather was Satan, or at least his second in command." My grandfather manipulated everyone, including my grandmother, my mother and my mother's second husband. I guess you could say he manipulated my dad because my dad eventually agreed to a divorce and he agreed to leave me with that tyrant my mother married. He manipulated me. Even now that he is dead, you would think I have peace. No! I can feel him in me. How sad is that?"

"I never understood why they hated my dad and I am still not sure how they really felt about me. I guess it's hard for women to hate their grandchildren, especially when there is only one. Although my grandmother appeased my grandfather, she tried to love me from afar as much as she could. She did a lot of things for me behind his back, even

...

taught me how to drive. Even though we lived in the same house, I felt my own mom loved me from afar too. There were times when I wondered if she blamed me for everything that happened to her. She and my grandmother were afraid of my grandfather, and as a result, normally followed his lead in silence. They let him and my stepfather punish me for things I did and things I didn't do."

"What do you mean 'things you didn't do.'"

"I heard him tell my mother my dad got her pregnant on purpose to spite him, and he should have left us with my dad living in the projects. My mom told him she would have been better off. One day he told me the same thing. When I told him I'd be happy to live with my dad, he called me a bastard. I was angry when he said that. I wanted to punch him in his chest, yelling, "I AM NOT A BASTARD," but I didn't because I knew he would take it out on my mother. I became so jealous of my friends that had great parents and grandparents. Even though I did not get to see them as often as I wanted, if it wasn't for my dad's parents, Papa and Grammee Martin and Abuelito y Abuelita Hernández, Marguerite's parents, I would have had no clue what grandparent love felt like."

"Wade, you always talk about your grandfather as if he never showed you any love, even to the point of referring to him as a hypocrite

or Satan. Are there any good memories about you and your grandfather?"

"Good memories? Um, no, ma'am. Well, actually, that's not totally true. We made wonderful memories when we weren't around each other. He was happy and I was happy. Like I said, he blamed my dad and me for ruining my mom's life and *his* plans for her. It was my dad's fault she got pregnant and it was my fault because I was born. Since he couldn't break my dad, he took it out on me. Most of the time, he was what you Shrinks would call a verbal and emotional abuser. An example would be if he found out I was going to visit my other grandparents or my dad, he would always try to talk my mother into changing the plans so I couldn't go. And when my mom went against his wishes, he would find a way to spite her for it.

When my mom was married to the lunatic, she stopped going to church because he was physically abusive towards both of us and no one, including her parents, stood up for us against him. My grandfather blamed my stepfather's abuse on me because I did not get along with him. He would call me a heathen/demon child. I could tell you many stories about him not biting his tongue about how he felt about my useless, unnecessary existence.

"Wade, we all have someone we would just as soon not be around. They have disrespected and hurt us in one form or another.

...

However, even the worst person has some good qualities. I'm sure if you allowed yourself to do so, you would remember some good times with your grandparents. It's not healthy…"

"Doc, let me stop you right there. I know your job is to find good in everyone. Heck, you are still trying to find good in me and you see me all the time. There are times when I don't think there's any good in me, but I'd like to think I'm redeemable, even when The Voices are telling me I'm not.

"My grandfather!" *Wade stood up and walked to the window, laughing and shaking his head…* "My grandfather felt he was the personification of Jesus Christ Himself; always right and everyone who disagreed with him was wrong and met with his wrath and threat of hell's fire. It didn't matter who you were. He was abusive. He would go to church and stand in the front, even in the pulpit sometimes, as one of the church leaders praying and praising God and then terrorize my grandmother from the moment they got into the car until the next time they walked into the church. He was the biggest hypocrite I've ever come in contact with, and I have met several self-centered-you-know-what's in my lifetime. However, the only person that comes close to him was my stepfather. As far as I'm concerned, they were just alike. My grandfather destroyed my mom and dad's marriage and then married her to Charles Manson. And no one could understand why I don't want to have anything to do with

...

God. What kinda God would tolerate someone like my grandfather and stepfather as leaders in an organization that is supposed to represent Him. I didn't want anything to do with them or Him. I still don't."

"Wade, I'm sure there is at least one good memory you have concerning you and your grandfather?"

The look in his eyes were as if he was in severe pain. He sat down and started pounding the palms of his hands on his temples, as if he was trying to knock something in or out of his head.

"Just please shut up for once in your lives! I don't need you to answer every question for me. *I know* who and what he was, not you! Just! Shut! Up! **PLEASE!**"

Then he was quiet, exhausted, still with his head in his hands. Slowly, he rubbed his hand over his eyes and then from the front to the back of his head, as if to wipe away whatever was there.

"I told you what happened at my graduation dinner, right?"

"Yes."

"A week or two later, my grandfather sent for me. He was no longer living at home. He was in a nursing home because my mom and grandmother could no longer care for him. He was terminally ill and had dementia. I really did not want to see him. Even though I was old enough to protect myself, I still didn't want to talk to him. My mother said it was important I go because he was on his death bed and I needed to see him before he died. Honestly, I would have been ok if he died without me seeing him or talking to him again. I guess she figured he had some words of empowerment to bestow upon me, like Isaac bestowing blessings on his sons. Ha! Yeah, right!"

"As soon as I walked into his room, he looked up from whatever it was he was reading and told me how I have always been a disappointment to this family even though it wasn't all my fault. He said I was just a bad seed. I had inferior genes in me. He said he did the best he could to purge me of those demon Martin genes. My immediate response was, "I'm fine grandfather, how are you?" Although neither of us could care less how the other was doing."

"I can still see his face as he sat there in his chair, looking up at me like he was Abraham or Moses or somebody else with God-given rights to bless or un-bless their children. I wanted to turn around and walk out, but I promised my mother, so I stayed."

"He said I made it difficult for him to ignore the defective Martin genes inside of me. He would love to believe he will see me in heaven, but we both know the probability of that is very low. He said God turned His back on me when I was born a bastard child. Me and The Voices laughed." Everybody, except him, knew he was not headed anywhere near heaven. The day he died, he went right back to hell

...

where he came from! But, what I said out loud was, "I don't care whether God likes me or not. However, I am NOT a bastard child; despite your efforts, my parents were married when I was born."

"I told him I learned in my psychology class that in order for an emotion such as hatred to continue to live, you must feed it every moment of every day with something…truth or lie…it doesn't matter. All of my life, I have watched you master this craft and I have learned to continually feed hatred. I guess I'm more like you than you want to admit."

"YOU ARE NOTHING LIKE ME!" he scowled.

"I laughed."

"I remember standing there, looking at this pitiful man who was supposed to be my grandfather. I wondered why he hated us so much. I could hear his voice, but at that point, I wasn't listening anymore until I heard him say, "You will never amount to anything." I looked at him and said, "You can thank yourself for that. You destroyed my parents and put your abusive demon in the place of my father!" You hated my father so much you tried to turn my mother and me against him. You did not care we were being abused by the man you gave my mother too. It's your fault The Voices live in my head. It's your fault that I hate God. It's your fault God

...

hates me!" Goodbye Grandfather! I walked out as he was preparing to say something, and I never went back."

"Three weeks later, he was dead. I thought his death would lift a heavy burden off of me; that I would finally be able to say my grandfather left me a legacy I can be proud of; some positive code I could live by, a reason to honor God. Again I ask, why should I have trust in a God who honors men as hateful and malicious as my grandfather was.

"Well, he passed no positive legacy down to me. This would not be an Abraham and Isaac moment. Even Ishmael got a better deal than I did. He left the physical and emotional scars of him "purging" the demons from me, the evidence, after all these years, still on my body and in my mind. He left me with Post Traumatic Stress Disorder because of the murderer he put in our house. I *still* hear him telling me how trifling my father was and how I was a *mistake.* The only thing his death did for me that might be considered positive was it removed him physically from my life. However, emotionally he is still in my spirit."

"Unfortunately, as I look at all the damage, I have caused and all the hate I have spewed out all over people, I'm no better than him. Actually, I'm worse because I should have been better."

(Note for future reference: I don't think Wade realized he acknowledged one of the reasons for the voices. Another first. We seem to be making progress.)

Before his session was over, the guards decided his session was up. As he walked out, he said,

"Come to think of it, there was one pleasant memory I have of my grandfather…The Car." *He nodded his head as he walked out,* "That…was the only good memory I have of my grandfather."

(Another note: I want to find out what he meant by this statement, and his earlier statement referring to his stepfather as a murderer. However, it seems the guards decide when the session is over, not me, the one with the mental health credentials! I will have to make a note to ask him when he returns for his regular session next week. And I will have to talk to the Warden about his guards…)

Chapter 8: Session 14
The Car

Once we had completed the preliminary chit-chat that occurs at the beginning of every session, I immediately recounted the conversation Wade and I had on his last visit, and I asked about his grandfather and "The Car."

"Out of all the traumatic events going on in the world, and all the stories I have told you about my family, the *only* thing you want to know about is 'The Car?' Seriously?"

"I'm curious as to why the only good memory you have of your grandfather… is a car?"

With a very sarcastic smirk, he said, "First of all, to clarify my statement, *he* did not give me the car. He died, which gave my grandmother the opportunity to officially give me her car. The car she promised me and the car he basically forbade her to give to me."

I suppose the look on my face was still questioning the correlation between him, his grandparents and this forbidden car.

"Let me help you before you give yourself a migraine. This is the story of 'The Car.'"

"My grandfather bought a brand new car for my grandmother. That in itself was a mystery. For as long as I can remember, if my grandparents were together, he always drove. Not out of chivalry, but because he didn't want her to drive anywhere without him in control of where she went and

...

when she went." *He rubbed his mouth, as if he was wiping away words he shouldn't say to me.* "Of course, my grandmother knew how to drive, and she has always had a car of her own. However, she only drove it to places he absolutely refused to go, or, whenever she would just leave him on the porch cussing and fussing because she wouldn't tell him where she was going. As a matter of fact, she and my mom taught me how to drive. I think as a rule, grandmothers should be Driver's Education teachers and teach teenagers how to drive. Five minutes in the car with my grandfather and 'Oh My Goodness!' It was horrible! I considered forgoing a driver's license and moving to New York or Atlanta, where I could get the city bus or subway anywhere I wanted to go."

"After she had a stroke, it was easier for him to "control" her movements. After her recuperation period, the doctor's cleared her free to return to all of her normal activities – including driving. My grandfather used her stroke as leverage against her driving and other movements. He told her he felt *more comfortable* chauffeuring her around so she would not get hurt."

Laughing, he continued, "He was the only one who believed that story. Hey, it was his and he was sticking to it. Everyone else knew the real deal. It was his way to stay in control. So, he always managed to come up with a reason why she was no longer "able" to drive her own car, although

...

she was quite capable. If my grandmother needed to go someplace, and he didn't want to take her, she would call my mother, or she would go with one of her church friends. He didn't like it, but what could he say, 'NO! and tell her can't ride with her daughter and friends' as if she were a teenager. When I got my license, my grandmother promised me when she no longer wanted to drive, she would give me the car. When I graduated from high school, she decided it was time, but he wouldn't allow it. His excuse was the car was *'too much'* for a teenager." *He shook his head.*

"Doc, you look at me as if no one person could be so horrific, and I must be making this stuff up to waste my time. Well, rest assured, I am not making him up. Someone in this building has my mother's phone number. Call her and let me know what she says."

"Wade, I see how you would feel he was mean and even evil. I understand. However, I have not heard anything that would warrant him being compared to Satan. Nor that would be a cause for you to distrust God."

He stood up, responding angrily, "Doc, are you not paying attention! I need you to review your notes! I *told* you how he treated my parents and me. I *told* you what a *blessing* for me looked like. I *told* you about that lunatic he made my mother marry. How can you NOT understand? I will tell you what I don't understand…I never understood how he could speak

...

the name of Jesus and treat us the way he did. He was the head trustee at their church, community representative with the city council, and a bully towards my grandmother, mother and me. He was the King of Hypocrites. You want to know why I turned against Jesus?" *Still angry, but now teary.* "That's why! My grandfather and my stepfather were demons who called themselves Men of God. They **told** everyone they were Saved, Sanctified, and **Filled** with the Holy Ghost. **NO ONE** being honest would say that about them. The only thing they were filled with was…" *He crimped his lips and closed his eyes. With a deep long breath, he continued,* "Doc, I have too much respect for you to tell you WHAT they were filled with! My stepfather was abusive towards me and my mother; my grandfather was mean and abusive towards us and my grandmother. He hated my father and did everything he could to keep me from him…which made no sense considering he hated me too. You would think he would be happy to send me to my father, but if he did, then my father would have won. And, he wasn't having that!"

(Note: Today, I saw a new side of Wade, anger plus defeat. He has not shown that combination of emotions during the last sessions. So, I just nodded in recognition of his words.)

After I earned my license, my grandmother would call me to come and take her wherever she wanted to go. Because they knew my grandfather would have a hissy, in the

...

beginning, my mom would come, and they would allow me to drive. After a while, I just showed up by myself.

After he got sick and unable to control everyone's comings and goings, it messed him up inside. He was still mean and ornery, but watching him shrivel to nothing, gave me a better understanding of what Nebuchadnezzar probably looked like when he lost his control over Babylon. You know who he is, don't you? I'm sure you all talked about him in school since he basically had a psychotic breakdown or worse. I consider both men to be kind of sad."

"Back to "The Car." The reason he said the car was too much for an eighteen-year-old was because it is a "Powder Blue - 1969 Ford Thunderbird 2-door Landau - Thunder Jet 429 V-8 Cruise-O-Matic - 2-door Coupe with Rear-Wheel Drive - automatic 3-speed gearbox. It cruised at 11.2 miles to the gallon – and most importantly… 0-60 in 8.1 seconds!"

(Note: Since Wade started with his sessions, I don't think he has had such exhilaration in his voice and expression as he did while describing this car. Pure Passion).

"My grandfather bought it brand new off the lot in 1969. It had 15 miles on it."

And just as quickly his smile faded into a frown…

"His real feelings, which he did not hesitate to tell me in private, was I was born a hood-rat, would always be a hood-rat and did not deserve anything as nice as this car."

He paused for a moment to recover and gather his thoughts after such a traumatic recollection of this season in his life. Then he smiled and said, "In 1977, when he died, the car was in mint condition. And guess what, twenty years later, it is still in mint condition!"

(Note: This was the first time I saw him excited and happy, and it was sad because, so far, the only thing that has brought excitement in his life was an inanimate object...a car. Hmmm)

Then his face clouded. "At least that was one thing I did not let The Voices mess up for me. I can truly say my relationship with Bird is the longest, positive relationship I have ever experienced!

The morning of my grandfather's funeral, my grandmother refused to ride in the family car. She gave me the keys to Bird and asked me to drive her to the funeral in *my* car. I hugged her neck, and she hugged me as if it were the first time she had ever hugged me. That's when I realized she was controlled by him, just like everyone else and she really did love me. I still had issues with her I had to work out. I felt because of her fear of him, she allowed so much hurt and pain to happen. And because of that hurt and pain, the loud voices woke up and have been the demons living in my head

...

ever since. However, that day, when they threw the dirt in his face, we were all set free from his tyranny. We happily sang that old spiritual, 'I'm free…praise the Lord. I'm free. No longer bound…no more chains holding me. My soul is resting. It's just a blessing…Praise the Lord, Hallelujah. I'm FREE!"

'Wade, you have said before it was your grandfather's fault The Voices live in your head. However, you have not explained why you feel that way. Whenever you are ready, we can talk about it."

Wade looked at me with a hollow stare, which made me feel as if I were looking into a deep black pit of emptiness. I could see the tears welling in his eyes and I could see him trying his best to hold them back. I said nothing. His time was almost up, and we sat in silence for about five minutes. Then he stood and headed to the door.

He turned and looked at me and said, "Dr. Stewart, I told you, my grandfather was Satan's twin and even in his death The Voices remind me I will never be worthy…NEVER! Doc, I really don't want to talk about him anymore. Talking about him gives me a headache, and, it makes *them* talk louder.

Chapter 9: *Session 17*
A Murderer's Funeral

Today is not Wade's normal visit. He missed two sessions after a very intense session about his car, his grandfather and the voices. He went to the clinic and told the nurse he needed to see me because The Voices would not be quiet. When he came in, his mood was dark. He sat quietly, holding his head the way he does when The Voices are talking. Finally, he looked up with distress in his eyes.

"The Voices won't stop talking! They talk when I'm awake and they talk when I'm asleep. They won't stop!"

"Did you miss your medication?"

"NO! Why is everyone asking me if I missed my medicine? How can I miss my medicine when that Nurse Johnson enjoys standing there watching, with that giant wart on her nose...have you seen it!"

Wade shivered his body as if he had a sudden chill.

Sounding like the Wicked Witch of the West, he mimicked Nurse Johnson, 'Ok Mr. Martin, it's time for our medicines. Drink lots of water now...you don't want us to choke now...do you...my prettie... **ha!ha!ha!ha!ha.***' DISGUSTING!!* I'd love to just ONCE *(holding up his index finger)*... JUST ONCE, I would love to puke those pills up all over her shoes!!!"

"Mr. Martin, Nurse Johnson is just trying to help you stay healthy and sane."

Wade smirked and rolled his eyes.

...

"Why do you think they are more active now than normally?"

"Who?"

"The Voices"

"Doc, I don't know why, isn't that your job, to tell me why?! I do know one thing…they are trying to make me lose my mind. I'm pretty sure they want me to commit suicide. *They tried before."*

"What does that mean, 'they tried before?'"

"They tried to make me commit suicide. They almost succeeded."

"When did they try to make you commit suicide? And. how are they trying to MAKE you commit suicide now?"

"They keep reminding me of all the bad things I've done. They keep saying if I had not done what I did in Beaufort, my father and Marguerite would still be alive. It was my fault she got sick…and it was my fault my dad had a heart attack…and it was my fault for everything. They said I should give everyone a break and leave… permanently."

"What did you say in response to their accusations?"

Almost in a whisper, Wade replied, "I told them they were right."

"They said I was right when I told my grandfather I was just like him. They said I was a demon child. They said I was wrong about my mother's husband. He just had issues he had to work out. I should have given him a chance. I just

...

ignored them because he was just like my grandfather. All of them are a bunch of demons and he was a murdering demon!"

"Were they talking in general or about a specific incident?"

"They said I should have been more *re-morse-ful* at my mother's husband's funeral. I told them if I had not thought it would have upset my mother, I would have danced at his funeral and…well, you know…on his grave! I didn't. But I wanted to!"

"What happened at the funeral that made you feel like dancing…and, well, you know?"

"He died…and he got away with murder!"

"I thought you told me he went to prison for attacking your mother and causing the death of your unborn sister?"

"And I told you he did not complete that piddly sentence they gave him. I told you how he wanted my mom to take care of him after he was released from prison because he was sick. I didn't want her to have anything to do with him, but she did anyway. She didn't let him move in her house; however, she did go to the nursing home to visit with him and to make sure he was being taken care of properly. Didn't I tell you all this before?"

"Yes."

"Anyways, whenever he was able, she would bring him to her house or out to dinner or something. Like they were dating…disgusting!"

"I remember you saying she did not file for a divorce…"

Wade cut her off, "So."

"He died about a year later. I remember when my mom called to tell me he was dead." *He shook his head, almost snickering,* "I thought…good riddance. Well, I found out quickly I had actually said it out loud because my mother gasped and burst into tears over the phone. I apologized, but it took her a minute to pull herself together." She said, *"No matter what he was or what he did, he deserves to be respected in death!"*

"I apologized again. She said he told her while in prison and in sickness he had repented of his sins and he had hoped I would have forgiven him." "I asked her was she telling me she forgave him for all the horrible things he did to her and to her baby? She was very quiet for a moment and then she said it was very hard; she had to pray for strength to forgive him, not for his salvation but for hers and mine. Like I said, my mom is a **S-A-I-N-T**… SAINT! I don't know if he repented or not. God was not having anything to do with me then, so I did not ask Him. I respected my mom enough to allow her to believe whatever she wanted to believe. Even The Voices were quiet on that. Now, they got too much to say!"

"The people at the funeral didn't know him. They couldn't have, not the way they praised him up one side and down the other, like he was John-the-freaking-Baptist or somebody. Not once did anyone say he was in prison because he was a wife-beater and baby murderer. Not once! I wanted to jump up and tell them all who he really was! I was sitting between my mother and grandmother and they both must have known what I was going through inside because they reached down at the same time and held my hands."

"This was the most vainest, possession-loving man I have ever known, and they chose the hymn, "Christ Is All." Doc, do you know that song…

"I don't possess houses or land, fine clothes or jewelry…" **FIRST LIE!**
"There are some folk who look and long for this world's riches…" **HIM!**
"There are some folk who look for power, position too…" **HIM AGAIN!**

"Wade, what about the rest of the song? Maybe the reason your mother believed he was repentant is because of the rest of the song…

"But I have a Christ, who paid His life, way back on Calvary. Christ is all, all and all, this world to me.'

It could be that he really did repent."

"Doc, pa-leaz! Give me a break! That man will **<u>not</u>** be waking up on the first resurrection…Even I know that much!"

"I looked at my mom while the choir was singing. She was crying silently. Tears were flowing down her face. I was in so much pain for her and the meanest of The Voices kept saying she will be crying over my grave soon enough!"

"What did you say?"

"Nothing. I made myself feel my mom and grandmother's hands on top of mines and I just sat there. I wanted to cry for my mom, but I did not want anyone thinking I was mourning him. So I refused to allow tears to fall."

"Well, I did snicker when the preacher preached him from the casket to the grave to heaven and back to the grave again. This preacher must not have read *any* word in any Bible. Even I know dead people stay in the ground and he was about to be dirt. There are no "souls" hanging out in white robes, floating on clouds or playing harps or walking-around-heaven-all day! And even if it were true he would be walking alright…on hot coals and brimstone hanging out with my grandfather and his other demon, hypocrite friends - in hell!

Just then, Wade practically jumped up from the chair with his hands on his ears yelling, 'SHUT UP! JUST SHUT UP! I

...

DON'T WANT TO HEAR THAT RIGHT NOW!" *Then he*
slumped back into the chair and cried, "Abuelita por favor,
Abuelita por favor ... haz que dejen de hablar ...por favor..."

"Wade, you are asking your grandmother to make them stop
talking...what are they saying?"

Dr. Stewart tried to persuade Wade to repeat what he was
hearing.

"I'm tired...I just want to go home now."

Once he was settled, I called for a guard to escort him
home...to his hospital cell.

(Note: The session did not end well, which is never a good
thing. The Voices are getting worst. They are getting more aggressive and
resistant to medication. And he is not able to hear Abuelita or The
Whisperers, as much anymore. He said when they talk, the mean, loud
voices drown them out, making it difficult to hear them. We will have to
search for the root of the voices, but Wade is not ready to face the
truth...whatever that is...)

(Update: Unfortunately, this prison's guidelines will force
inmates to take their medication, but will not force them to attend
therapy sessions, unless it's mandated by the court, a problem I am
working to rectify in the near future. Medication alone is never an all-
inclusive or adequate therapy technique. The only way to help any mental
health client is with both medication and therapy, especially severe cases
like Wade Martin.

Because my cases are with the most critical inmates, I choose to
send notes to remind them of their appointments and urge them to attend.
Wade ignored my notes. He missed two appointments before he
returned).

...

Chapter 10
Even Stable People Have Unstable Moments...

Something in one of Dr. Tiffany Parker-Stewart's client sessions triggered uninvited memories from her past. She was feeling very emotional and decided she needed an appointment with her private mental health coach, who was very familiar with 'outside' of her story. Today, Tiffany knew she would have to do what she continually urges her clients to do...she would have to allow herself to deal with the inside of her story...the part she wants to ignore...the darkness.

"I told you about the "counseling" sessions my parents insisted I have with their pastor because they thought he could talk me out of my boyfriend and choice of majors. When I refused to agree to see him, my parents still forced me to see him. They assured me they would be with me, and if they couldn't come, there would be someone assigned for supervised visits. They made it seem as though I had a choice, so I reluctantly agreed."

"When they told the pastor it was not feasible for me to travel back and forth, he was *too* willing to come to my school, and even pretended to agree with the supervised visits. I purposely scheduled the sessions in very public places like the library, counseling center, student lounge and campus chapel. He tried to cover his hatred for my choices of meeting places by saying, due to the nature of our conversations, we should meet in a more private area. I told him that would not be necessary because I had nothing to say to him that was private."

"After about four meetings, I refused to continue the sessions. When my parents asked me why, I told them it was inconvenient. He was aggravating. It was interfering with my classes, study time and whatever else I should have been doing, as opposed to wasting my time with him. I did not tell them he was touching me and smiling and saying inappropriate things to me.

"Why didn't you tell them what he was doing?"

"I knew his insistence for face-to-face sessions was a ploy to find a reason to get me alone, for 'counseling,' which I tried to tell them, but as before, they wouldn't listen. Later, my mother told me that even though she couldn't quite put her finger on it, she felt something wasn't quite right about his terms for the sessions. But, she did not do anything or say anything, not even to my father. Unfortunately, by the time my parents realized the mistake they had made, it was too late. Eventually, that "something" my mother was feeling revealed itself. The damage was done, and their religious doctrines could not help them repair me."

"Anyway, my parents were upset I refuse to see him anymore. My father threatened to take away financial support, thinking I would relent for the money. Now, I am very knowledgeable of Bible promises and curses and I knew if I

...

disrespected my parents, it would not go well for me. So, as politely as I could, I reminded my parents I was attending school on a full academic scholarship with everything important paid until graduation, so I was willing to find a part-time job, so I had money for incidentals."

"In other words, they attempted to bribe you. Well, it does works for most college students!"

"Yes, but not for me. With everything that was happening between my parents and me, I was very close to severing my ties with them and my faith, which was not in my original plan. I did not want to be in the same church where he was pastoring and I wanted to pursue the career I believed God had for me, within my faith. However, between my parents and their pastor, my decision to sever ties with the church was a decision solely based on the pain, church-hurt…a hurt my parents help to fuel."

"When my parents withdrew their financial support, I maintained my grades in both majors, while working part-time to help support myself. They were furious when I refused to go to their church when I came home during spring break."

"Tiffany, why were you so leery of the pastor? Had he done or said something to put you on alert whenever he was around?"

"He had been the Pastor of their church for about five years before I left for college. From the beginning, I

...

never really cared for him…not from the first day he was installed. There was something in my spirit that could see his demons. Because of what I felt, I was always uncomfortable around him. Even when my parents, his wife or the entire congregation were present, I always felt he was looking straight through me and not in a discernment / pastoral sort of way."

"Several of my girlfriends and I talked about how he always seemed to stand too close or look at us too long or say something that seems to be outside the realm of a Pastor-to-young lady church-member-conversation. Even though we mentioned our discomfort to our mothers, several times, nothing was ever done – never said. One of my friends, who was a year older than me, told her mom he actually touched her. They changed their membership to another local church, but still, nothing was done – nothing was said. I mentioned one incident to my parents when he was completely in my personal space and commented on how *nice I looked* in my dress. My mother tried to say he was just complimenting me. When I told her his tone and look was more than complimentary, she literally got angry and the conversation that followed helped me to know my parents would not tolerate me "talking disrespectfully" about the Pastor. So, I didn't say anything to them about his continued advances towards me."

...

"Whenever I was home, he would ask me about school and ask me questions pertaining to my personal life – what I do in my free time…and with whom…did I have a boyfriend and how did we spend our time. Stuff I felt was none of his business."

"I accepted a summer internship in Seattle, Washington, as the assistant to a forensic psychologist. It was the perfect opportunity for me at the time. I was highly recommended by one of my professors and it was on the other side of the country, far from my parents, their church and their pastor. They had made up their mind about me and my boyfriend, so why bother. I had not lost my faith in God; however, I had decided I didn't have time for a church that believed God allowed heathens and hypocrites to represent Him and His church."

"I'm sorry to keep interrupting you, and (Ha!Ha!), I'm about to ask a question that is really none of my business, but, that's what we do, right? Why did your parents consider your boyfriend to be a 'heathen'?" I understand your faith has a strict belief that being unequally yoked, as it is described in 2 Corinthians 6:14, means not being in a relationship with someone outside of your faith. However, why were they so against **him.** *"*

"No problem. Sometimes, we just gotta be nosey in order to make sure we are keeping up, right. Ha! Ha!.

...
86

The problem for them was that my boyfriend was Muslim. He was raised Muslim. His parents were also concerned, but they did not treat me the way my parents treated him. Well, to be honest, my parents had not met him. Also, neither my parents, nor his, knew he had begun to study with me from my Christian Bible. We started out using my Sabbath School lessons and compared the scriptures with the Koran and the Christian Bible. I learned a lot about the Muslim faith, and he learned a lot about the Christian faith. After a while, we were using, by his choice, the Christian Bible more than the Koran. He was conflicted about the differences between his beliefs and my beliefs. I remembered a book I saw in the library entitled 'Sharing Christ with Black Muslims.' I checked it out for him to read. I think that book helped to make up his mind to consider conversion to Christianity. I personally did not have a preference in his decision. At the time, the severed relationship between my parents and I, and my faith was not a positive example for him. Nevertheless, I let my parents think what they wanted to think. I never told them he had chosen to convert."

"The next downfall for my parents was my church membership being removed without any explanation. They knew I was hurting; but, they would not try to understand how I could turn my back on the church, religion and maybe, even God. This was another presumption of theirs because I

...

never told them I was turning my back on anything, or that I was changing my membership. They just assumed, because my name was no longer on the church membership roster, that I took it off and I was turning my back on God."

"The hardest thing for them was my refusal to talk to them about anything. They could not understand what was happening to me, because they did not know what *had happened to me.* I would not discuss it and whenever asked, I would get very agitated. My mom later told me she suspected my sudden change had something to do with the sessions with the Pastor, but she was afraid to voice it out loud. My father could not shake the disbelief he felt the day he was told I had removed my name from the church membership. Normally, as a church leader, my father would have been privy to this sort of information in advance. However, he wasn't. When he questioned the pastor, the explanation was that it was a last-minute decision by me, who, as an adult, requested my parents were not to be involved. My father's vast experience as a church administrator and his knowledge of church policy made him suspicious of what the pastor said, but he, like my mother, did not follow his instincts."

"My parents watched me work to maintain my grades for two majors while never knowing I suffered silently in pain."

...

"One day, unbeknownst to me, my boyfriend called my father. He did not waste time with chit-chat because he knew they did not approve of him. He started the conversation by saying he was concerned about me. He told my father he had been away on his residency and I was fine when he left. However, when he came to visit me he could tell immediately something happened and he could see it eating away at me, but I wouldn't talk to him about it. He knew it had nothing to do with him and he suspected it had everything to do with my family, the church and that pastor. He said my father tried to interrupt him in protest, but he continued to talk. He told them between work and school, I was only getting a couple of hours sleep a night and he was worried I was making myself sick, not because of the work or classes, however, because I was using all of my emotional power to move past whatever was bothering me. He told my father if he could fix what was wrong, he would have, and never had called. He also told my dad if he finds out someone has hurt me...only Allah will be able to protect whomever it was. If he did not have to leave, he would have taken care of me himself and not called them at all. Unfortunately, he had to go back to Charleston, and he was worried about what I might do. He told my dad he hoped he looks past his dislike of him and takes a concern about my physical and mental

...

health. He said he did not even wait for a response. He just hung up."

"*Really, WOW!*"

"Yes."

"That weekend my sisters were in town, so they and my parents came to my college to spend the weekend with me. Before they all left, they begged me to tell them, or someone else I trusted, what was wrong, what actually happened to me. I wanted to tell them, but I was afraid they would turn against me or somehow blame me, so I didn't. That night I woke up from a terrible nightmare, crying and begging God, if He loved me at all, to please tell me what to do."

"The next day, I called and met with my sisters and told them what happened. They were mortified and told me if I didn't tell our parents, they would."

"The story of my anguish was nowhere near what any of them thought was wrong. They were hoping I was being convicted by the Holy Spirit because of my lackadaisical attitude about my faith. Or better yet, my boyfriend had proven to be the wrong choice for me, as they had warned, and we had broken up. They were devastated, as I figured they would be, because the real story was not what they were ready to hear."

"I visited my parents the following weekend and I told them the entire story."

"After I declined further sessions with their pastor, he showed up at my dorm room door, unannounced, in person, alone. My roommate was out of town, my friends were all someplace else and my boyfriend was in Charleston completing his residency. I decided since they were all away, I could use this time to just relax. I had on shorts and a tank top and was listening to some nice jazz when the knock came to my door. I opened it because there was no reason not to. It would have been awesome if it had been my boyfriend. Instead, I was shocked to see *him* standing there. The look on his face told me this was not going to be a pleasant visit. I tried to close the door, without saying anything to him, but he pushed it open and walked in, smiling, as if I should be happy to see him. He tried to hug me, but I stepped back, out of his reach. He did not waste time with niceties. No 'hello,' 'how are you?' 'how are your classes'? None of that. He looked me up and down and the smile on his face told me he had demons doing the thinking for him, you know that creepy look grown men give young women. Finally, he said he knew I had been avoiding him. Now that I'm all grown-up, I should just give in and admit what I knew to be true…that I wanted… *him*. He reached for me, but I moved. I'm sure you remember how very small dorm rooms are, especially one full

...

of furniture. As I watched him, I was also scanning my room for empty space I could use to get away from him. He told me if I refused him, it would not go well for me. He reached for me again and I moved away picking up my cellphone. He stood there for a moment, still smiling, unbuttoned his jacket and then sat on my bed, as if he expected me to sit there with him. The only solace in the entire ordeal was the fact that, even though he was stupid enough to think threatening me would help me want him to touch me, he was also stupid enough to let me get between him and my door."

"You know, once I started telling my parents what happened, I could not stop. My mother was crying and the expression on my father's face was none like I had ever seen before. My anxiety level was so high I could hardly breathe. Even now just telling you the story…just recounting that horrible time and everything that happened ten or so years ago, remembering what I had hoped was long forgotten, my anxiety level is still high, as if it happened today."

"Do you want to take a break, get some fresh air?"

"No, I'm fine. I don't think I had ever been so scared. All I kept thinking about was my boyfriend respected me enough to respect my virginity and this scum was trying to take it from me. However, I refused to let him see my fear. I stood there, glared him squarely in the eyes and told him I would gladly live in prison for *the rest* of my life before I

...

allowed him to put his filthy hands on me. I told him the people of that church, including my parents, may be ignorant enough to think he was God's man, but I knew he was straight from Satan and the pit of hell and he would visit him that day if he attempted to touch me again! I gave him an ultimatum, remove himself from my room immediately or security would be escorting him to jail. Not a threat …a fact. At first, he did not believe me until I hit the 9 - then the 1 – and the last 1. He was, of course, furious, but he left my room. Just before he exited, he told me I would regret this day. And I thought, so would he. What he didn't know, is my phone was on record the entire time. I love my phone!"

"Yes, they do come in handy for more than Facebook and Crush Candy games."

"I told my parents I guess, at his first opportunity, he called an emergency meeting of the church board; of course, when my dad was not present. He told them I was converting to Muslim and I wished my membership removed permanently from the church records. Because everyone in the church was either in fear of him or thought he was God sent, no one insisted proper administrative procedures be followed. When I received the notification my membership had been removed, I knew what he had done and at that moment I didn't care. Good riddance to bad rubbish! I just let everyone believe I voluntarily removed my membership."

...

93

"When they could breathe normally again, my parents asked me why I didn't tell them then. I reminded them of the times I told them about him and how they made me feel. They accused me of making up lies, and that it was sacrilege to imply their pastor was anything less than a Godly man. I just assumed they would have taken the pastor's side. I said, "After all, I'm becoming a psychiatrist, I'm dating a heathen and I'm becoming a heathen…your words, not mine.""

"At that point, everyone was in tears and furious. My dad was pacing the floor with a look and posture I had not seen on him before. My mother just shook with tears of grief and anguish. My parents have been so protected in their faith, they had no clue how to react to what had happened to me…their daughter, and by whom…their beloved pastor.""

" I love my parents, and I knew they loved me. However, by this time, I was happy letting them keep their God and their religion to themselves. I was done. I was exhausted and without even waiting for a response from my parents, I went to my room and locked the door. I had no more talk in me. I slept until almost noon the next day."

"When I finally came down, I expected to be alone in the house, but to my surprise, my parents were sitting at the kitchen table with their family attorney. Mothers being who they are fixed my plate and sat it in front of me. I wanted to resist, but I didn't because I was starving!"

...

"To my surprise, my parents had done something totally unexpected. They did not talk to the pastor. They did not call a church board meeting. They called directly to the conference president, the pastor's boss, and told him everything I had told them. They were waiting for a call back from him as to what the next step would be. Their attorney told me that regardless of what his employers do, they had a civil lawsuit and he is ready to process it when I was ready.

My parents told me how much they loved me, and they were sorry for making me think otherwise. They are very sure about their religious beliefs, but not to the detriment of their children. They left the decision of my faith, my career and my relationships to me, with a caveat that I allow them to be an active part of my life. Of course, I was in agreement with their request.

The pastor's employer's legal team's investigation revealed many complaints about this pastor, not only from their church, but from previous churches as well. He was fired from the conference. His license as a minister was revoked, he was charged in civil court by several families and his wife divorced him."

"The conference reinstated my church membership, although I still wasn't sure if I trusted God enough to trust His leaders. As for my boyfriend's threat, I told him if he went anywhere near that man, he would have me and Allah to

...

answer to. In court, he made eye contact with him whenever he could to let him know his life was in danger."

"I completed my Bachelor of Arts in Psychology and my Bachelors of Science in Biology, both, with honors. I was accepted into a neuropsychology graduate program in Charleston, six hundred miles away from my hometown. I felt the distance was crucial to maintain a healthy relationship with my family. I knew if I studied at a university near their home, my parents would continue to poke their fingers into my life, which would upset everyone. Also, my soon-to-be husband accepted an assignment at the Naval Health Clinic in Goose Creek, South Carolina with an opportunity to study oncology with an emphasis in oncology research at the Cancer Center in Charleston."

"I chose to specialize in neuropsychology in graduate school. Doing a project for one of my classes, I acquired an interest for acute brain trauma victims that are incarcerated. During my studies, I had an opportunity to complete forensics classes and mentor under a forensics psychologist who worked in the mental health ward at a local prison. I graduated with a master's degree in Neuropsychology with an emphasis in Forensics, and my Doctorate in Brain and Cognitive Sciences. While in graduate school, I worked for the correctional custody system, including juvenile detention. After graduate school, I received my first position as a prison

...

psychologist, while completing my medical degree in psychiatry."

"I married my college sweetheart immediately after completing graduate school. He was excelling as a naval doctor and oncologist researcher, and I was becoming a very successful psychologist, if I do say so myself. I started my own practice where I worked with all types of clients and completed mental health evaluations for prisons, lawyers…and sometimes even families. We now have the American Dream…three children, two girls and a boy, a dog, a cat, a parakeet and some goldfish. Oh and yes, the white picket fence."

"Blessings come in all shapes and quantities. So, how is it that you became the deputy director of the mental health center?"

"Several years after completing my psychiatric degree and working within the state prison system, I was offered an opportunity to create and manage a pilot program for a full-service mental health center in South Carolina. It was decided to house the pilot program in one of the prisons without a functioning mental health presence. In this particular prison, thirty-five percent of their inmate population was diagnosed with a major or minor mental disorder upon entry into the system. It was suspected that another thirty or forty percent were undiagnosed, which is not good in any organization, but especially not in a prison environment. The doctors and

...

therapist available were contracted in from the state department of mental health with a client ratio of 1:75 and saw inmate clients once every two months…maybe."

"I was very excited about the opportunity. I agreed to work part-time while developing the pilot, setting up the administration of the counseling center, hiring licensed counselors, psychiatrists and social workers, and re-diagnosing every inmate. When we launched the pilot, I came on full-time for one year in order to guarantee the success of the project."

"Obviously the program and the center continues to be a success. We have become the model for centers in several other prisons, in and out of state."

"We still utilize the contracted staff for the minor mental health cases with a therapist/client ratio of 40:1, which is not horrible. This frees up my team to work with the major cases; and our client to therapist ratio and lowered to 35:1 and they see their clients at least twice per month. I am very proud of what we do…making a big difference in the lives of the inmates."

"I now have an assistant deputy managing the day-to-day functioning of the center, which gives me the opportunity to go back to my own practice. I now come in two or three days a week to maintain stability as the deputy. I assigned myself some of the harder mentally challenged inmates. Thus

...

my encounter with Mr. Timothy Wade Martin and his accompanying "Voices," as well as, other clients like him.

There is one thing I have learned while working in the prison system. All the mess I went through in life brought me to this point…at this time. What happened…has happened. But what will happen is entirely up to me and I try to instill that concept in my staff and in my clients.

Chapter 11: *Session 18*
Half And Half…

Doctor Stewart motioned for Wade to sit. He chose to stand…

"So, you've talked about your grandparents and your parents, however, you have not really talked about your siblings. I do remember you referring to your younger brother as "half and half." What is that all about?"

"Ha! Really!? It's quite simple. He is my half-brother. My father's child and he is half Black and half Hispanic. So, Half and Half."

Wade sat down, shrugging his shoulders and sucked his teeth to indicate how dumb he thought the question was.

"Antonio has always been a thorn in my side. As the oldest, I felt Antonio received privileges our dad should never have offered him. What was amazing about the entire situation was, no matter what I did, he just kept coming back. Whenever I visited my dad, Antonio wanted to be around me and hang out with me. Regardless of how mean I was to him, he kept coming back. He loved me no matter what and I wish I could have hated him…but I didn't…and I still don't. I just wish he had never been born."

"Everyone was so excited. Augh!! Until they came along, I was the only recipient of Grandma and Grandpa Martin's affections. Until I was twelve, they did not have any other grandchildren – just me. Even though I didn't get to see them as often as I wanted, they were my safe haven, until the babies came."

"YES," rolling his eyes, "you heard me right…I said BA-BIES! Twins…two of them. Born April 19, 1968. Don't even ask me why I remember their birthdays. Ha! Ha! I guess it was a traumatic experience for me. At least one of them was a girl, Maria. She was kinda serene. She was the kind of kid that didn't let much bother her, but when she had had enough, anybody in her way was in trouble. And, she has not changed, still full of vinegar. And then there was Antonio. Geez-Louise! It was like having an infant Tasmanian Devil around. He was not destructive, just totally aggravating. I remember once I told his mother, Marguerite, he needed medicine. Ha, as you can imagine, that did not go over very well. She was very upset that I would insinuate he might have a "problem." Something *was* wrong with him. Doc, he never sat down or shut up, and, even as a child, he was neat to the point of obsessive. I like stuff clean and where it belongs, but he was ridiculous…HA! He still is. I have no clue how he survived boot camp and living on a ship with slobs."

"I have to give Antonio his props though. He was a very smart kid, except in math. He was as dumb as a rock when it came to math. I tutored math in high school, so when I was around him, I was able to tutor him which helped our

...

relationship a little…a *very* little bit." *Wade pinched his fingers together to show how much a "little bit" was.*

"Marguerite, my dad's wife, always treated me like one of her own kids. I don't know why she did that, maybe because she knew nobody else loved me or maybe because she came from such a loving family. I'm sure she knew how bitter I was, and I think she knew about the voices. Since Marguerite was Hispanic, she spoke to her children, and me, in Spanish so that we would be bi-lingual. Also, most of her family only spoke Spanish, so we all became pretty fluent in Spanish."

"Antonio became fluent enough to become an interpreter. That's what he did to make money in high school, college and while he was in the Navy. I wish he had stayed in the Navy or stayed someplace. If he had, I wouldn't be here, because my dad would have turned the business over to me, instead of that…" *Wade rolled his eyes as he crossed his legs in the opposite direction and folded his arms across his chest.*

"Wade, why do you have such malice in your voice about your brother and your family business? You said you didn't hate your brother; however, your tone seems to differ. Why don't you tell me the real story behind these feelings?"

"You know, Doc, you ask too many questions!"

"Thank you for acknowledging I am doing my job…asking questions that will help me understand you and help you help yourself. So, again…what are these feelings all about?"

"When Antonio was young, I felt as if I had to compete for my dad's and grandparent's affections. I never had to do that before. Despite everything going on in my house, I knew my dad and his side of the family loved me and wanted to make me as happy as possible. After he moved back to the States, he tried to protect me from my grandfather and stepfather. Whenever possible, he would bring me to visit wherever he was stationed. The best time I had with him, as a child, was when he brought me to Puerto Rico to be his best man when he married Marguerite. I was eight years old."

"As we got older, my dad didn't recognize how he was catering to Antonio over me, which I know was coincidental since they lived in the same house, but I didn't care. Since I was the oldest, I guess they all thought I would adjust with no problem. And I probably would have if I had allowed myself to do so, but I didn't."

"The straw that broke my back was when he revealed he intended to, one day, turn MMTrucking over to Antonio and me. It should not have mattered, however, deep down inside, it didn't sit well with me, sharing the business with him. As a child, I had to share my family. As an adult, I had

...

to share my money. I was not happy at all and the madder I got, the louder The Voices got. Eventually, I lost all reason and started doing everything I could to sabotage Antonio and the business, not realizing it was killing my dad…I was killing Marguerite and my dad."

"Wade, how did Marguerite die?"

A sadness came over Wade's face, "She had cancer."

"Are you saying you feel responsible for her cancer?"

"No, I'm saying it was my fault. No one paid any attention to her health. They were all trying to figure out what my next move was going to be."

"My dad and Marguerite tried their best to help us form a good family bond. They took me on as many vacations as possible, especially when they went to visit her family in Puerto Rico. I looked forward to going there and getting loved on by my Abuelos. Plus, there were hundreds of cousins and aunts and uncles … just a lot of family. It was the only time I was surrounded by so many family members. And to make it better, they all wanted to be around me."

"The last time I went there was when my Abuelo died. Marguerite and Dad didn't go because Marguerite was very sick, and he refused to leave her. He loved her more than oxygen. How can anyone love somebody that much? It's not logical."

"Anyways, my dad asked me to go to the funeral with Antonio to represent him and Marguerite. I remember thinking, 'What the…, why would I want to go anywhere with him.' The good thing was Antonio was already in Puerto Rico, so I didn't have to fly five hours with him. One of us would have died before the plane landed. It had been sad enough missing Abuelita and now Abuelo. I just did not have the desire to spend a week with Antonio. It wasn't because he did anything. Just the thought of him breathing got on my nerves, because I knew the day would come when he would be the boss over me. I know just how Esau felt."

"I'm sorry, what has Esau to do with all of this?"

"So, are you telling me you don't know who Esau is?"

"No, I know who Esau was. I'm just wondering why you compare your life with his."

"Oh, I was about to worry. I'm supposed to be the demon child; I can't have my shrink be a heathen too. Ha!Ha!

"Ha!Ha! Very funny, sir. Carry-on, please."

Anyways, Esau gave his birthright away for beans, literally. And then his blessing and heritage was stolen from him by his greedy brother. You know the story. Antonio did not steal my birthright. My dad gave him my birthright, MMTrucking. A few years back, I told Antonio to just buy me out, but he wouldn't do it.

"In the story, Jacob tricked his father into giving him his brother's inheritance. Am I correct?"

"Yes, but…"

"Did Antonio trick your father into passing the business to him?"

"No, but…"

"So why do you say Antonio took…"

"Doc don't try to confuse me. I already said what I had to say. I was capable of running MMTrucking. I'm the oldest. I should be in charge, not that…"

"Even though we haven't talked about what brought you here, you do remember why you are here…what you tried to do…don't you?"

"The only thing I did was try to take what was already mine. If my dad had done the right thing and if Antonio had not blocked me out, I wouldn't have met you. Do you know, they went so far as to have spies watching for me and they would call him to let him know I was on the property. Before I could even walk around good, he was calling my phone or walking up on me. Do you have any idea how nerve racking that was? Like I'm some sort of thief or something!"

"So, it was first your father's and now Antonio's fault you are in this predicament. They cooked up this plan to portray you as someone they needed to protect the family business from?"

"That's not what I'm saying…"

Wade stood up and started pacing the floor and rubbing his head the way he does when The Voices are yelling.

"So Wade, what are you saying, because if I'm not mistaken, you tried to bankrupt the company. So I'm just trying to understand…"

Wade cut her off , "Doc, don't put words in our mouth…GUARD! GUARD! I'm ready to go…"

The guard looked at me for confirmation. I nodded my head to let him go.

Chapter 12: *Session 19*
The First Time...

"Last night, in my nightmares, the Evil One reminded me of the first time I almost left here. He said he *almost* had me, but my dad and his Jesus interfered. He just laughed and said another day will come...very soon..."

"*Wade, in your nightmares whose voice represents the Evil One and what happened that "he almost had you..."*

"There was a time in my mid-twenties when I felt like everything in my life was falling apart and I couldn't catch the pieces to put them back together. I was the literal Humpty Dumpty and when I fell off the wall, there was no one willing to even try to put me back together. I will admit I had burned so many bridges and alienated myself from my family because of what I believed to be the truth."

"My dad had basically fired me because he said I put the entire business and family well-being in jeopardy. So much drama! If he had done what I suggested, none of it would have happened in the first place. It's not my fault the man wasn't on the up and up...how was I supposed to...anyways, their precious company wasn't in any danger anyway."

"*You are really talking in circles right now. Is it because you don't want to tell me what really happened? And is what really happened the reason you wanted to leave?*"

"I hired Christopher Gregory and I knew he was shady…"

"*Isn't your collaborations with Mr. Gregory part of the reason you are here now?*"

"He got himself locked up because he was stupid and careless on the highway. Even an idiot knows to follow the rules if you are transporting drugs, especially across state lines. And I told him to call me if anything went wrong." He got his stupid behind arrested with an unlicensed weapon on him. Idiot!"

"*And you say you did not know you had hired a drug dealer. Obviously, you knew exactly what was going on; nevertheless, you allowed your family to believe you were innocent in all of this…*"

"Doc, **do you want to know when I tried to kill myself or not**! I don't want to talk about all this other stuff. Next thing I know, you'll be agreeing with them!"

"*Very well, you may continue, however, we will revisit this. What happened that made you feel like the literal Humpty Dumpty?*"

"Like I said, after all of that mess, *somebody* thought I had the drugs, which I don't know why, since *I was exonerated* for having anything to do with it. My name or fingerprints were not on **ANYTHING**; and, I didn't have any drugs

...

109

since they were confiscated by the police. Any idiot knows if there's a drug bust, the drugs are confiscated by the police!"

"My dad put me on a *(Wade crunched his fingers on both hands in the universal sign for quotations)* "leave of absence" if I agreed to go to drug and gambling abuse sessions at some rehab joint he knew about. It was run by one of his Navy buddies and they had a very good success rate. If I refused to go, he would fire me, so of course, I went."

Well, one night, about three weeks afterwards, I was walking from my car and a few thugs jumped me, dragged me into a nearby alley in between restaurants and beat me pretty severely. They said the owner of the drugs sent them to teach me a lesson, but they were not allowed to kill me…that would come later. Well, they didn't kill me, just broke my leg and some ribs. I told the police and my family it was a crackhead with a baseball bat trying to rob me."

"*And they believed you?*"

"What choice did they have…there were no witnesses. In reality, no they didn't believe me and neither did anyone else. Regardless, that was my story and I stuck to it!"

"Well, while in the hospital, the Evil One helped me to realize something very ugly about my life. I knew I was always acting irrationally, and I was always making excuses for my behavior. I knew The Voices, especially the Evil One, was always talking me into trouble by making me mad about

…

something. You know what's really crazy… hmmm…, the majority of the time Antonio was overseas someplace with no plans to come home anytime soon. Nevertheless, I allowed myself to be obsessed with jealousy and the thought of him taking over. I was too dogmatic to listen to my dad or change how I felt. I let them help me ruin a lot of things in my life."

"When you say that, what in particular comes to mind."

Wade looked out the window. There was sorrow in his voice…

"Like the only girl I loved, period. Since then, I have had no one I could consider a love interest. While I was at home recuperating, I realized there was really no reason for me to even be in the situation I was in. Actually, I stayed in my dad's boarding house. He had a room, just for me, so it wasn't like I was not being cared for. My family was there every day, except Antonio because he was overseas someplace. He called whenever he could. They all made sure I had everything I needed. Esabelle was studying to be a nurse, so she used me as her guinea pig. She changed my bandages, took my temperature and blood pressure and made sure I took my meds. You would have thought I was still in the hospital. There was no logical reason for me to feel unwanted and unloved. I let them tell me my family was just pretending to care about me and they were all hoping for the day when I wasn't around, and they would all be better off

...

and happy. Well, I started feeling really bad for myself and then anger towards them."

"Then the Evil One started telling me I should just put them all out of their misery, especially since I was such a troublemaker and an embarrassment to the family. I was broken and unrepairable and it was really all their fault. The Evil One just wouldn't be quiet. I tried to tell him to shut up because I was in pain and I did not feel like listening to him; my leg was killing me, my arm was killing me, my head was killing me, everything on me hurt. I was about to call for someone to bring me some pain pills when he showed me where Esabelle had put them. I took two, because everyone knows you take prescription pain pills two at a time, unless you want to overdose."

"I took the two, but I was still hurting. It felt like someone was stomping around in my head and stomping on my leg. I don't ever remember being in that much pain. So, I took two more. Then the Evil One told me to take two more to stop the pain quicker."

"Remember I told you about The Whisperers. I could hear them saying don't take anymore, but the Evil One was screaming at them to shut up and mind their own business. 'Wade, take more, take them all and the pain will go away.' Then I could hear screaming, but not from The Evil One and the other voices. It was from outside of my head.

...

Then I saw darkness, but I could still hear Esabelle's voice and the conversation like it was yesterday...

"Wade, Wade what are you doing?"

"I hurt everywhere!"

"Why didn't you call me?"

"He said the pain will go away if I take two and then two more and then four and then more…"

"Who said to take two and take four?…Wade who told you to do that?…"

"Then I saw bright lights shining in my eyes and more people calling my name and moving me from my bed to something and then I was racing so fast I couldn't breathe. Then it was dark again."

Esabelle asked again, *"Who said to take two and take four…Wade who told you to do that? There was no one here!"*

"I woke up in the hospital a couple days later. My dad, Marguerite and my mom were there. As I looked around the room, I noticed my leg in the air.

"How did my leg get up there?" My dad told me I took twelve of the pain pills before Esabelle came into the room. He said I walked on my broken leg to where Esabelle had put them on the other side of the room on the dresser. I broke my leg again, only worse. I told them I did not remember any of that. I just remember horrible pain."

Dr. Stewart interrupted Wade, *"Did you answer Esabelle's question?"*

Wade ignored Dr. Stewart and continued with his story.

"I was in the hospital for several days. One day my dad told me I said the Evil One told me to take the pills so I wouldn't feel the pain anymore. I told him I did not know what that meant. My dad said something I have never forgotten. He said Satan's plan was to steal my joy, kill my spirit and destroy my chances of salvation. At the time I didn't want to hear any of that because I was formulating a plan to get even with street rat Christopher Gregory.

"Now, after the fact, do you believe your father to be correct? Do you believe The Evil One is Satan, trying to snatch your soul?"

"I don't care nothing about that. I listened because I was in pain and unable to walk out on my own. It's not important anymore, and, since me and God are not on friendly terms, I don't have time to worry about stuff like that."

"Eventually, you will admit you don't have to allow The Voices to tell you what to do and you do it, as if it was the best advice. How did you explain away the Evil One to your dad and Esabelle?"

"I told them I didn't know what they were talking about and it must have been the drugs talking. And yes, if Esabelle had not come into the room, I wouldn't be standing here listening to you telling me to explain to you why I didn't

...

tell them. And no, the Evil One is not my grandfather. If he was the Evil One, it would be much easier for me to fight him."

"Why do you think you could have more control if the Evil One was your grandfather. You said over and over he basically terrorized you until he died."

"The Evil One was in my head before my grandfather died. It's not him."

"Then, who is it? At some point, you will have to say his or her name out loud. Only you can choose when that will be. The longer you wait, the longer it will take for you to heal."

"I have to go now. I'm tired. Have a nice evening Doc."

"Wade…"

"See you, Doc."

Chapter 13: *Session 20*
Family Fun

"Wade, the last few sessions have been pretty stressful for you, so I thought today we would talk about something light and happy."

"Light and happy you say… are you going to tell me I'm being released, and I can go home."

"No, nothing that dramatic. I would like to hear about a time you remember having family fun."

Wade frowned and rolled his eyes.

"With what family? Family fun? Don't you have to be part of a family in order to have family fun?"

"What do you mean…what family? Your family. I know your family has had some fun times, birthday parties, game nights, barbeques, family vacations…something you have participated in. So, not including your father's wedding, talk about a time you actually had fun with your family."

"When I was a teenager, I lived with my dad and his family in California. That, and my graduation, was the only time, since the wedding, I really felt like part of a family. We were always doing things, having family adventures, as my stepmother called it. My dad was an instructor on the naval base and sometimes he was away from home for the entire weekend. Marguerite, my stepmother, always made sure there was something fun to do. Because I was older than her kids,

...

sometimes they would let me do teenager stuff with my friends. You know what, I did not mess up the entire time I was living with them. The Evil One was not living in my head then, so it was easy enough for The Whisperers to help me stay straight."

"Did you tell your father or Marguerite about The Whisperers?

"NO! Of course not! I wanted to tell them, but I was scared."

"Of what?"

"That they would send me back."

"Send you back?"

"To my mom and grandparents. Back to unhappiness." Being there with them, even with my little nagging butt brother, was the best time of my life. My dad and Marguerite really acted like they loved me."

"Acted like?"

"I don't believe many people truly love me, except maybe Rebeca, and I told you how that ended."

"What other things do you think were better during your time in California?

"I was always pretty good in school, especially math, but I did very well in the school I went to on the Navy base. I was on the honor roll every year. Marguerite praised me all the time because I could help the twins with their homework.

I made friends and I was actually sad to leave there and return to darkness and misery.

"Hmmm…" Wade turned and rolled his eyes at me…

"What?!... Doc, I know that "hmmm." It means you don't like what I said, so…what would you rather hear!?

"I'm just observing and listening…"

"I remember we went to this resort for a whole week. My dad let me bring one of my friends. It was wonderful. We had a curfew, but we could do pretty much anything we wanted as long as we didn't leave the resort. I even let Antonio and Maria hang out with us for a few hours every day. We would go to the pool, to the arcade and to the cantina. There was even a free movie theater. There was so much to do, and it gave my parents some time to themselves."

"You wanna know what, the only school friends I had were the ones I met in California – Navy Brats, like me. California was the only time I had friends over for anything. It's funny the things you remember.

"Why didn't you keep in touch with them?"

"We kept in touch for a little while. If you know anything about military, families move around every three or four years and it's easy to lose track. After a while, I didn't have time to keep up with people."

"You might be able to find them on Facebook, if you like."

...

"I guess. Somebody would have to help me. I never had time to learn Facebook."

Wade stood looking out the window at the inmates playing basketball...

"You know, I don't have any friends, not even in here. I have no family...no wife...no children. My brother and sisters hate me. My mom is upset because I won't let her visit me. Hmmm, if it weren't for you and The Voices, I'd be completely alone. Oh, and let's not forget Nurse Johnson...I think she has a thing for me," Wade laughed.

Wade laughed for a moment. Every now and then he lets the sunshine in so he can experience a little bit of life's humor. This was one of those moments. Even I had to laugh with him on that one.

I walked over to the window and stood next to him...

"Wade, you should go out there and play basketball with the others..."

"Doc, the last time I went out there, it was a disaster. I wasn't even playing, and my anxiety level flew off the charts. They were arguing over who had the ball, who touched the ball, who was supposed to have the ball and who was supposed to pass the ball to whom, blah! blah! blah! And, I saw at least four fights...well almost fights in the little bit of time I was out there. I told the guard to let me back inside. I went to my room and went to sleep."

...

"Look", *as he waves for me to come back to the window,* "they are arguing out there right now. No offense to you, Doc, but I'm trying to get out of this joint. I'm counting down the days. You know that church song… *Wade sings the song…*

"Count the years as months… Count the months as weeks… Count the weeks as days, any day now…I'll be going home…"

"Ha! Ha! You forgot I could sing, and I knew a few church songs, didn't you! Ha! Ha! Ha! Well, I do, but I'm not talking about going to heaven, like in the song. I'm talking about gettin' up outta here, on time, without any problems. I'll miss you Doc, but gotta go…gotta go. Thank you very much."

Just as quickly as the happy moment came, it left and there was a look of sadness on Wade's face. "Anyways, Doc, back to our original conversation. Other than Puerto Rico and California, the only time I had family fun, is when my fun did not include my family. I annoyed them and they annoyed me. I went to mandatory family functions and I usually came late and left early. It was easier that way. Less opportunity for The Evil One to take over my part of the conversation."

Chapter 14: Session 21
When It's Your Fault...Who Do You Blame?

Today I had plans to continue our conversation about Wade's distrust of his brother and why he continues to refuse to see him when he comes to visit. However, when he walked in, he barely said hello before he blurted out...

"Did I tell you I was the reason my dad had his first heart attack and maybe the last one?" I did not tell my family about the voices. Well, I think I told you I tried telling my mother and grandparents. My mother was concerned with protecting herself from that maniac she married, so my problems took a back seat. My grandparents refuse to listen to me talk about hearing voices. Demonic is the word they used over and over when they were describing me. This was just one more symptom of demon possession. I never told my dad or his parents. Weirdly enough, they were quiet when I was around my dad's and Marguerite's parents. They made me yell at my dad that day in his office and..."

He was standing in the window. He slumped down on the floor under the window and began to sob.

"Dr. Stewart, I killed my dad because I was selfish and hateful. My family is very angry with me. Not because of what I did, but because of how I treat them all. The really

...

ridiculously strange thing is they still love me, after what I did and after how I treat them. What is that all about?

He sat under the window. The tears continued. He was silent for about ten minutes.

"I told you about the years I lived with my dad. I was a teenager. I lived with him and his family in California for three years."

"In 1969, my Dad was promoted and transferred to become an instructor in the construction mechanic school in Port Hueneme, California, where his career first started. My mom gave my dad permission to take me with him to California for the three years they were stationed there. It gave me an opportunity to have a true relationship with my sisters, my stepmom and even my brother. Considering I wasn't used to having babies around me 24/7, I did okay as a big brother. I also was beginning to realize my Dad really did love me, really did want me and really did want the best for me. I learned being angry all the time wasn't going to change the past or help me progress into the future."

"When I was living with them, I could see my dad treated us both the same. When I wasn't living with him, I was so jealous of the relationship between him and Antonio. The Voices kept telling me he favored Antonio over me. The more my dad tried to reassure me the more paranoid I became."

...

"Anger is cruel and fury overwhelming, but who can stand before jealousy?"
Proverbs 27:4 (NIV)

"About six months after Marguerite's death, I had a terrible argument with my dad about the business. I basically told him to give me my financial share of the business since he didn't trust me to run it. Then I would leave MMTrucking and the family alone for good. While we were arguing, my dad suffered a heart attack."

"Maria accused me of trying to kill **her** father. I remember her yelling at me asking me why can't I just be happy? Doc, I wasn't trying to kill **my** father. And before I could ask him for forgiveness, The Voices told me I didn't need to care about him because he didn't care about me. If he was dead, as the oldest I'd get everything. I mean, I called for help, but…" *Wade cursed under his breath…* "I actually thought about it for a second, what they were telling me to do. Then I yelled back at Maria telling her he was my dad first and how dare her to insinuate that I tried to kill him. I refused to admit, until today, that his heart attack was my fault. I let The Voices make me a murderer. No better than my mother's husband. I should be in here for murder.

He sat on the floor, under the window, with his head in his hands…and cried. He is finally seeing who he allowed himself to become while blaming it on everyone, with every voice, except his own.

Chapter 15: *Session 22*
Who's The Boss…You Or Them

"Wade, it's time to talk about The Voices … for real."

Wade rolled his eyes and sucked his teeth. He remained silent for a moment.

"Why?"

"Because as long as you ignore the real cause of all of your life mishaps, you will never resolve them. You have had a rocky life and a major part of your life is your voices. If you want to be in control of your own life, you will have to confront The Voices and the control you gave them over your thoughts."

"They are not **MY** voices!"

"They are yours as long as you continue to hold on to them.

"I already told you about the first time I heard them, when he was killing my mom. I would hear from them off and on after that. When my dad asked me to go with them to California, The Whisperers told me it would be good to get away from the mess for a while, and to spend some time with my 'other' family.

"The Mess? What were they referring to?"

"Anyways…," *Wade paused long enough to imply he was ignoring the question…* "I remember telling The Whisperers if they were determined to live in my head they needed to make sure I made the honor roll every semester for as long as I'm in school. They did. Even high school and college. I think that was some sort of silver lining…what do you think Doc?"

"Hmmmm, I suppose that is one way of looking at it…"

"When I was a senior in high school, I worked as a math tutor." *Wade paused, blew on his fingernails and rubbed them on his chest…* "Yes, I had some smarts back then. I was tutoring this little nerd kid. He was always talking about Jesus and all the stuff he did at his church. It was weird enough they went to church on Saturday, however, to be eleven years old talking like a preacher, was annoying, to say the least. He was always trying to introduce me to Jesus. I told him I already knew Him, and I did not have time for Jesus and Jesus did not have time for me. His sister was in a couple of my classes. She was gorgeous. Well, she still is. She set it up for me to tutor her brother, however, she basically told me she didn't really like me because she felt I was cocky. *Smirking,* Huh…me…cocky? I don't know where she got that from *(laughing).* I asked her to go to the junior prom with me. She didn't go because their mom was really sick, cancer. I wanted to be angry because I felt she used her mom as an excuse. The Whisperers told me to get over myself.

"Whatever happened to the boy and his sister?"

"Their mom died. The boy, his name is Jason, turned against God. He eventually became an accountant. The reason I know that is (*Wade smirked)* because his sister joined

...

the Navy and met my brother. She eventually married him. Now we are all one *big happy family*."

"Anyways, The Whisperers loved me, and I guess I loved them too. They protected me from intrinsic and extrinsic harm. Ha! You didn't know I knew words like that, did you! Nope, you didn't."

"I'm impressed. You seem to have many jokes today. That's good. However you are still avoiding the inevitable."

"I can't stand up to the Evil One. It's too hard and he's too loud. He, along with a group of loud voices, showed up and have ruined my life ever since. The other shrink…oh…sorry, psychiatrist, told me with my rage and low self-esteem, I keep them fed and employed while making their job so easy. I'm guessing you agree."

"That is a good analogy."

"Why do you feel the Evil One showed up when it did."

"I…don't want to think about the Evil One. He's been quiet for a few days and I don't want him to wake up and start yelling."

"The Whisperers have always been the only constant in my life. That's sad, don't you think? The only constant friends I have are voices living in my head."

"Do you remember I told you about the girl I loved. Her name was Rebeca. I have not heard from her in about twenty years. She would have been good for me. When I met her, I was planning how to fight Antonio."

"I guess me **and** The Voices had an agenda we were not willing to allow some girl to disrupt. If she had stayed, it would have been the end of them and the end of my vendetta against Antonio. And this crazy life I have lived probably would have been much different. The sad part is when I let her go, I knew actually what I was choosing and what I was giving up. I needed the strength The Voices gave me to combat my family. Continuing to love her would have been a distraction. For some strange reason, she has been on my mind lately. Besides Doc, if it weren't for me sticking with The Voices, you would not have met me!"

"Wow, what a loss that would have been for me."

"So, you have been comfortable allowing The Voices to be in charge of you. You say The Voices are the stimulus for your jealousy and anxiety towards everyone, but especially Antonio. You say The Voices are the cause of your continued paranoia. Wade, you must decide if you want to be in charge of your life or if you want them, specifically, the Evil One, to be in charge of your life."

"Don't smush my words all around Doc, like you are playing some scramble word game! They are not in control of my life. I'm in control of my own life. I decide what I will do and what I won't do, NOT no voices. I'm the boss of me, heck, I'm the boss of them!"

...

128

"Why didn't you tell anyone about the voices."

"I did not want them to put me away, take my share of MMTrucking and forget about me.

"What makes you think they would have put you away?"

"What do *you* think? I was hearing voices and having weird thoughts. I became more and more paranoid about their intentions, even my dad's. I knew my dad loved me and wanted me to be a part of this family and the business. I knew that, but I could tell they were conniving behind my back. I always had to be a step ahead of them… a step ahead. *Wade stood up and took a big step in front of him.* "Yes, ma'am, a step ahead of them because the easiest thing for them would have been to have me committed."

"What you have to admit, if you want to heal, is that your jealousy and anger proved to be detrimental for everyone, including you."

"I don't want to talk about this anymore. I'm tired and my head hurts.

"Wade, not talking about them will not make The Voices disappear. They will remain 'the boss of you' for as long as you allow them to control your thoughts and your actions."

"You keep saying that! They don't control me! Why do you keep saying that! They don't make me do anything…"

...

Wade had been standing in front of the window and at that point, he slid down to the floor and held his head in his hand. I sat on the floor with him.

"Wade how many times have you said The Voices enticed you to do or say one thing or another? If you are the boss of them, then how would that have happened. You have to look back and find the exact time you were so afraid of them you handed them control of your life, rather than fight them. You have to determine why you thought it was important to keep them a secret…and no…it wasn't because you thought they would lock you up, because, you and I both know that's not true. When you can identify and admit these things, then, we can start the healing process. Until then, you are just spinning your wheels and they will continue to be the boss of you, instead of you being the boss of you."

Wade stood up, and then helped me up. He walked to the door…

"Doc, you are asking for a lot. I don't have the energy to discuss any of it. My head hurts and The Evil One is yelling, not talking, not giving instructions, not badgering, not degrading me…just yelling."

"He does not want you to hear what I have to say. Wade, Satan does the same thing. He yells at us loudly so we can't hear the Holy Spirit giving us instruction about one thing or another. Even you know and understand that…"

"I don't know if I'm coming back…"

···

"That's your choice to make. However, you have to decide who's the boss, you or them. If you want it to be you, then you will be back. Whether you believe or not, read 2 Timothy 1:7. Read it in the King James Version. Whenever I see you again, you can tell me what this verse means to you."

"You always wanting me to read something in that bible of yours." Isn't there some government law against making people read that bible?!"

"Yes, however, I am a Christian Psychiatrist, which they knew before they hired me. And, I am not 'making' you read it. I'm just asking if you would. If you don't, then you don't. However, the Bible is the best road map ever written. It will always lead you to where you are supposed to be, if you follow its directions."

Wade sucked his front teeth as if you had something stuck in them…then took the note from Dr. Stewart's had and shoved it in his pocket.

"I'll think about it."

"Thank you."

Chapter 16: *Session 23*
Fear Is A Hungry Beast…

Wade did not return for three weeks. Then, he sent a note that said, "They told me they were in control and the Evil One was the boss of me." When he walked in, he looked as if he had not slept or eaten since the last time we met.

"Doc…"

"Wade. How are you?"

"Not good…"

"Because…"

"They would not shut up! It's your fault."

"I'm sorry… my fault?"

"That's right! He wanted to make sure I knew he was the boss of me. But, yesterday, something very strange happened. The Evil One was yelling, saying I was dumb and that I was always dumb, and he was the boss of me. Then all of a sudden…he stopped…they all stopped. Then, in the quiet, I heard a voice I had not heard in many, many years…

"Wade, you gave them control before you even knew they were there. It's not your fault Baby. It's his fault…it's my fault. I should have fought for you and I didn't…I'm so sorry. But now, you must fight…there is no more time Wade…you must fight…now!"

Wade's voice was choppy, and he was forced to hold tears back. He paced the floor…

…

"I couldn't hear her anymore. I begged her not to go. I kept calling her and calling her and telling her he said he was in control. He knows I'm afraid of him. I want to be in control, but I don't know how. She said, *"Go see the doctor."*

"Then silence. Then yelling… **'SHE CAN'T HELP YOU. That doctor can't help you. She has her own issues to worry about! You are so dumb you can't even see she don't care about you! You are just a paycheck for her!'"**

"I called for her, but she couldn't hear me over the yelling. She was gone."

"He kept calling me names, but I sent you the note, anyway. I can't live like this anymore. It's too hard."

"Did you recognize the voice?"

"Yes. It was my grandmother."

"Do you know what she meant by "You gave them control before you even knew they were there," and "I should have fought for you"? You know what she is referring to, don't you?

"It's too strong. I'm too tired."

"You keep saying 'it's' too hard. What or who is 'it'?"

"I have been afraid all of my life. I have been fighting from the day I was conceived. A child should not have to fight for love and recognition. A child should not have to be afraid of what will become of them. I've been telling you all, all this time, nobody loved me…not even my parents. I mean,

...

they tried to love me and protect me, however, most of the time they were trying to protect themselves from him. My grandmother tried to love me, but she was just trying to survive in a house occupied by demons. When my grandfather died, it was as if she started to breathe for the first time in 50+ years. Can you imagine being married to a demon for fifty years?"

"You asked me why I didn't tell them about the voices. Because I was already being treated like an urchin. I didn't want to put up with pitiful, as well. And yes, I used them, The Voices I mean, I used them for ideas to push out Antonio and push out Rebeca. I thought I was in control of them, but…"

Wade eyes darkened. He started rubbing his head which meant The Voices were talking. Then he started talking, not to me, but to the voices…

"You are **not** the boss of me! I'm the boss of me! *(Wade was hitting his chest with the palm of his hands.)* I don't care what you say… you made everybody hate me…even God!"

"Wade, who is talking to you?"

Wade stood up and paced the floor, from the couch to the window…from the window to the couch. Back and forth, rubbing and smacking his head with the palms of his hands.

"It's all your fault. You ruined my life. Ya'll ruined my life!"

"Wade, who are you talking to? Say his name…"

"No!"

"I can't! I won't! He is the Evil One! If I say their name, I will die. Don't you know he is trying to kill me! Don't you know that! Didn't you hear my grandmother say that…don't you even care…they are trying to kill me. Maybe he was right. Maybe you don't care…maybe it's all about the money…maybe, he will kill me anyway."

Wade slid to the floor, under the window, with his arms wrapped around his knees as he rocked back and forth.

Crying he said, "Doc, don't you see!? If I say his name, I will die and burn in hell with him! Even though God hates me, I don't want to burn in hell."

"Wade, is that why you refuse to go to any of the religious services or speak to the Chaplain? Because you think God hates you? God does not hate you. Remember the scripture I asked you to read on your last visit? 2 Timothy 1:7(KJV). Did you read it?"

"Yes."

"What did it say?"

"Something about the spirit of fear…I don't remember!"

"It says, "For God hath not given us the spirit of fear; but of power, and of love, and of a sound mind."

Wade chuckled, "Well, obviously whoever Timothy is isn't talking about me because I don't have a sound mind! If I did, I would not be here!"

"Wow, that's the first smile I've seen today. Good start. What does this text say to you about you, Wade Martin?"

He rolled his eyes at Dr. Stewart, "You really get on my nerves…I hope you know that! If I thought God cared anything about me, I guess it would mean there is no reason for me to be afraid of anyone. He wants me to think He's got my back! But, I know He don't. Because if He did, I would have grown up with my real father and mother, not that lunatic my mother married. You know, even though her father was evil, she did not have to divorce my dad and marry that man. She was an adult. She could have said no. It is her fault too I'm here."

"You take pleasure in pointing blame in every direction but towards you. In every decision you made, you had a choice. Go right or go left. You chose. No one chose for you. It is time you placed the blame where it belongs. The text says, '…but of power, and of love, and of a sound mind.' You have the potential to acquire these positive traits. You have chosen to utilize the negative traits you were taught by your circumstances."

"I am an old man. I have nothing to show for my life except misery and pain and heartache. Ok, so I *may* have brought some of it on myself. The Whisperers say I allowed

...

myself to fall into the trap and they could not help me get out because I didn't want to get out. They said I have to help myself. So, I helped myself by trying to help myself take what was rightfully mines. Look what happened to Esau. I did not want to be hanging out there looking like a fool because my little brother stole my birthright."

"Did Antonio steal your birthright? Because based on your history…"

"What-Ever! It don't matter how he got it, he got it, and I don't."

"Wade, until you are ready to acknowledge your contribution to your misery, The Voices will continue to live in you. Until you are ready to acknowledge your need for a divine intervention, The Voices will continue to be the boss of you. Until you are willing to acknowledge what you have done, the real reason why you did it and ask forgiveness from God and the people you have hurt along the way…you will live in darkness and misery. You want to be the boss of you…then take control of your life back from The Evil One."

"It's too hard…"

"Well, you are the only one saying that. I'm not saying…Antonio is not saying…and God is not saying. Only you. The first step to any twelve-step recovery program is to admit your issues and then admit that you are powerless, on your own, to defeat them."

"I don't want to talk anymore." *He walked to the door and banged on it with the full strength of his fists.*

...
137

"GUARD! GUARD! Take me back home!"

I nodded to the guard to take him.

(Note: Until he is willing to admit why he is here, in this prison, seeing me, and he is ready to admit his part in creating the darkness in his life, and most of all, until he is ready to admit who the Evil One is... he will not recover and more importantly, he may not live to recover.)

Chapter 17
Akina's Story

Akina Meets Phyllis

"Grandma!" *Akina was running up the steps. Then, as an afterthought, she caught her breath and put her hand to her mouth in surprise and almost in a whisper, she apologized,* "Oh, I'm so sorry, I did not think to ask what you wanted me to call you. I'm so sorry."

"Darlin', learning about you brought the type of joy to my heart that can't be described in words. I don't know if your aunt told you, but when she told me who you were and showed me your pictures, I cried for a moment. Wade is my only child, and under the circumstances, I've lived all of these years without a grandchild and now, here you are, my beautiful granddaughter. When I saw the pictures, I could see Wade and Rebeca in you. Calling me Grandma definitely works for me if it works for you."

In tears, Akina hugged her grandmother for the first time. "Grandma, I don't think I will ever get tired of hugging you!"

Phyllis beamed as her heart overflowed with love for this young woman, whom she just met, who, without a shadow of a doubt, is her granddaughter.

"Let's have a seat in the parlor. I have some treats and tea there for you. Now, you tell me all about yourself. Start from the beginning."

...

"My Aunt Opal told me to tell you 'the truth, the whole truth, and nothing but the truth'! So I will tell you as much as I know and then you will know the truth that I know. Is that okay with you?"

"Of course child, but first let me pour you some tea because I'm sure you are parched after your trip!"

"Thank you. The trip wasn't that long. It was a nice drive. I love this house. It is so beautiful."

"I used to live right there where your college is, however, when my father died, I moved here to take care of my mother. This is the house I grew up in, and, your father grew up in."

"Well, Grandma, the story of Rebeca and me could be a book all by itself. Even though my mother was pregnant with me while in graduate school, she worked as a photographer for local magazines, newspapers, and public television. She was an awesome photographer. You probably have seen some of her work in magazines and such, and just had not paid any attention to the by lines. Rebeca was really fabulous with a camera. She used to tell me she was shocked when, right out of graduate school, she was hired by the Public Broadcasting Service in New York City. I was three years old".

Akina sighed as if there was pain while she was thinking.

"Aunt Opal told me, years later, they all agreed it would be best for Rebeca to leave me with them instead of moving me to New York right away while she was getting settled. I think they all knew I would never really live with my mother and I would be better off growing up in Atlanta."

"*I see,*" said Phyllis with a questioning look on her face, "*Why do you call her mother sometimes and then 'Rebeca sometimes? It is not customary for children to call their parents by their first name, especially their mothers.*"

Akina sighed, "Sometimes, she was my mother, and sometimes…Rebeca was not."

Again, Akina sighed as if there was pain in her words. She continued telling Phyllis Rebeca's story.

When my mother chose my name, Aunt Opal said she told her there was a woman very special to her while she was in college. She always loved her name, Phyllis. Aunt Opal added Akina, which was my great-grandmother's name. My grandparents, (Rebeca's parents) were drug addicts and were not involved in her or my life. Aunt Opal is my mom and my mother's mom."

"*Yes, I could sense the maternal instincts in your aunt. I thoroughly enjoyed meeting her. She and I will be great friends. We had some very serious conversations about the Martin Family, and obviously about your father.*"

"Auntie Opal said, Rebeca's job took her all over the world. She was shooting pictures in countries most people only saw on TV. She and her partner, who was a journalist, made several documentaries. It…"

Phyllis interrupted her…

"You know, I do remember Wade asking me did I remember her. He had watched a PBS program where her name was listed as one of the photographers. I remember how strained his expression was as if it pained him to remember."

There was a momentary pause as if neither knew how to recover from that thought.

Akina broke the silence, clearing her throat.

"Could I please have some water or some more tea or something?"

"Oh my goodness!" screeched Phyllis as she hurried towards the kitchen, "Child, I was so engrossed in your story, and the fact that you even exist, I did not notice the pitcher was empty! I tell you sometimes my old brain deceives me!"

Akina followed Phyllis into the kitchen and sat down at the table.

"It turned out Rebeca and her partner were more than just work partners. They got married when I was ten years old. They were known around the world as the power couple in photography and journalism. However, they were *never* referred to as power parents. On occasion, during summer breaks, my cousin Michelle and I would travel with

...

them someplace. It was exciting to be able to tell the class I spent part of my summer in Japan or Germany or Costa Rica or Mississippi." *They both had to laugh about that.*

Phyllis said, "What in the world is there to film about in Mississippi!" They would have been better off coming here!"

"Well," Akina laughed, "There was always Elvis!" *They had a good laugh about that.* "Seriously though, they went there for the Blues Festival and Elvis Birthday Celebration a couple times."

"Even though he wasn't my real father, I really loved my stepfather and he really loved me. We had fun together and he tried his best to be a good father to me. However, he and my mother traveled the majority of the month, every month, while I lived with my aunt and uncle. His niece, Michelle, became like my big sister. She and I were in the same situation. He was her guardian because her mom died, and her father was never in her life either. She was in boarding schools and then college. She was two years older than me, but several times a year, she came to Atlanta to visit and we traveled together whenever possible."

The Accident and Memorial Service

Phyllis noticed Akina's smile slowly fade from her face and the light dimmed just a little in her eyes.

"What is it darlin'?"

"I hate my mother kept me from you. We could have had so much fun together. You would have been able to come to my prom and my graduation, and to the memorial. Two months before my senior prom and my seventeenth birthday, Uncle Barnell heard the announcement about a plane flying from Kenya to London that lost contact with the air control center. A few hours later, it was announced the plane crashed with no survivors. He knew they were on that plane. He told Auntie and together they had to tell me my parents were killed in the plane crash. Michelle called me. We cried and cried over the phone. Grandma, they had planned to take Michelle and me with them to Kenya, but the trip schedule was changed, and I had final exams. The day after the crash, a telegram arrived confirming my parents were passengers on the plane and that no one survived. It was horrible."

Akina cried and her grandmother held her for a while.

"As if we weren't already devastated enough over the accident, his family was upset because he did not want a traditional funeral service. If there had been remains, my parents wanted to be cremated without a religious service. They both left explicit instructions concerning their cremation and services, which was actually a party, and had already paid for everything in advance.

...

Even though there were no remains, his sister and brother were trying to get a court order for a traditional religious ceremony. Whatever religion they were, but he wasn't, forbid cremations and insisted on full length funeral services, in a church. He did not do church and said there was no reason to put him in one when he's dead, but they were bound and determined to disregard his wishes."

"What kind of religion…what kind of people…?" Phyllis frowned.

"I don't know. My parents did not talk about religion and his family never really liked my mother and me, so it was easy to blame his decision on her."

"Grandma Phyllis, do you know what was really funny? He told me once he knew they would buck his wishes, so in his letter, he said he did not care about their religious rules and no one could change his wishes. Then, he had his lawyer notarize it and file it at the courthouse. Their faces were **SCRUNCHED**! when I got the papers out of the safe and handed it to them."

They both had a good laugh.

"Since they couldn't have a "real funeral" the process was further held up because the adults, mainly his people, could not settle on a date for the memorial. After a while, I could not stand the back and forth, so I went to spend a couple nights with Michelle and just asked Auntie to call me and let me know what they decided."

"The service was lovely, and many people had a lot of nice things to say about them. I didn't say anything. I just sat there with my auntie and uncle and Michelle. We were glad when it was the next day."

"Akina, we can talk about it later if you want, but you said your parents did not talk about religion. Why do you think that was?"

"They taught Michelle and me about Jesus and heaven and hell and good and evil, the sort of stuff parents teach their kids and hope they don't turn into heathens because they didn't go to church. You know what I mean?"

"Yes darlin', I know what you mean. So far, it looks to me as if you have not turned out to be a heathen!" They both laughed…

"They did not believe in organized religion. They said religion was organized by hypocrites trying to get their point across."

"But my Auntie Opal and Uncle Barnard were very spiritual. It was sometimes comical around our house because my auntie is a crisp, hallelujah shouting, Amen Corner, head of the Usher Board at her church. She did not play when it came to church, not even a little bit. And on Sunday morning, don't let her have to tell you to get up. Oh my goodness!"

"My Uncle wasn't much better. He was the Choir Director and Pathfinder Leader at his church. He goes to church on Saturday. She goes on Sunday. There were plenty weekends I spent in church, night and day, the entire weekend! Oh, my goodness! I actually preferred Uncle Barnell's church, however, I went to both. I learned the Bible and all its interpretations, which made my parents happy…because they didn't have to teach me."

Insurance and the Reading of the Will

"A couple weeks after the memorial, and my graduation, we were all called together, with my parent's lawyers, for the reading of their wills. Auntie said they all decided it was best to wait until after my graduation, so Michelle nor I would not have this added stress before final exams."

"**Out of the blue**, my mom's brother, uncle and cousin, all looking like they had just been raised from the dead themselves, showed up at the reading."

Phyllis, trying not to smile, asked, *"Did they call you or come to the service."*

"Grandma, no, they did not. They *claimed* they had an "unforeseen delay" and could not make it to the service. Rebeca's parents would have shown up, but they were already dead and the reason I know that is because I remember going with Auntie and Uncle to the funerals. My mom and her husband met us there. Neither time did Rebeca shed one tear. Her family knew how wealthy Rebeca was because they were

...

always asking her to pay the rent, light bill, fix a car or get someone out of jail AND pay for the lawyer."

"How did they know about the reading of the will?"

"Who knows. I sure did not tell them!"

"They insisted they had a right to sit in on the reading of the will because they 'just knew their sweet sister broke them off a piece of something.' Grandma, it was awful."

Phyllis's eyes were watering trying not to laugh.

"Regardless of their faults, my parents were very good with their investments and had financed very well. Auntie and Uncle used to say they were 'very well off.' I used to overhear the grownups saying since they didn't have time for us, at least they made sure Michelle and I were well taken care of. Ha! Ha! of course I wasn't supposed to hear that, but I was a nosey child…Ha!Ha! By us being their only children, they were able to provide handsomely for me and my cousin Michelle, during their life, and now, in their death. They had already paid for our college and graduate school and bought us both a house, mine in Atlanta, where they stayed whenever they were in town. Michelle's house was in New York, although now she said she may not live in New York since her uncle was no longer there. I hope she moves to Atlanta."

"Anyways, back to the story. Because they traveled so much, my parents always purchased an extra insurance policy for accidental death. The policies were two million dollars

...

each. No one knew anything about the policy, not even Uncle Barnell and Auntie until the lawyers read their wills. We were all in shock. Their beneficiaries were each other, then my mother had me as her second beneficiary, with Uncle and Auntie as my trustees. My father had Michelle as his beneficiary. Because she was twenty-two and about to graduate from college, she did not need a trustee. My parent's investment company assigned personal finance officers for both of us to help us learn how to wisely budget and invest our money and the other investments they left us. They were there to make sure no one took advantage of us…like my mother's people. My mother told me they were all trifling leeches and could not be trusted. She said they would suck the air right out of your mouth, if you kept it open too long – but that's a whole 'nother story.'"

Phyllis could not contain herself and they both had another healthy laugh to brighten up such a gloomy state of events.

"The wills were very specific, so it was easy for the executors to separate the estate between Michelle and me, and the estates were portioned as designated in the will. Rebeca had a separate account set up for Uncle Barnell and Auntie Opal."

"When her people realized there was no free money and they could not swindle any out of me, they left, of course, very furious. They said they planned to sue for their right to a

...

portion of my mother's estate, vowing to have a lawyer contact us immediately!"

"Grandma, you know it's kind of sad, but not surprising, since there was no money to get, I have not seen or heard from them again. It's been two years. I guess they are still working on getting a lawyer." *More laughing.*

Akina became quiet with a sad-angry expression on her face.

"I think the saddest realization of my parent's death was that they would miss all of the important events in my lifetime. They had missed recitals and such before, but I never imagine they would miss the rest of my life. I really wanted to skip my senior prom and graduation, however my best friend and Michelle convinced me my parents would want me to go. During both events, I was overwhelmed with both sadness and happiness. Auntie and Uncle were fabulous and I'm glad I have those memories. Even as a young child, I knew my mother chose to leave me so that she could further her career. Nevertheless, I loved her and my stepfather. In their own way, they had the perfect relationship and they loved me and Michelle very much."

"Auntie Opal's friend from her church was a counselor. I did talk to her for several months during the summer. Michelle talked to the counselor at her college. She took it very hard because first, she lost her mother, and now she has lost the only father she has ever known. Her birth

...

father didn't even show up for her mother's funeral. She told her counselor she expects, if he's not dead, that eventually she will hear from him once he realizes how wealthy she is. So far, he has not appeared. After the party, we were sitting on the porch and she said that now she is officially an orphan. We hugged each other and we both cried for a while. I understood her pain because I felt the same way."

"My counselor told Auntie it was understandable that the news of my parents' death would send me and Michelle into a state of depression, and it would take some time for us to recover from it. She told her there was no set time period and all that can be done was to pray and be there for us."

"Michelle and I stayed in counseling for a while."

The Safety Deposit Box

"The second shocker was that Rebeca left a safe deposit box in their bank. Aunt Opal had a key. She never asked her what was in the box. Her instructions were that it could not be opened until I was twenty-one, unless she died, then Aunt Opal could open it to determine when I should be privy to its contents. Auntie went to the bank, alone, to see what was in the box. There was jewelry, foreign currency, her first check stub, old passports, her first camera, all of her journals and some old savings bonds addressed to me."

"What really surprised her were the pictures of someone she had never seen before. The pictures were of

...

Rebeca and a tall, dark, very handsome young man. They clearly seem to be in love. Why were these pictures hidden with her journals and why had she not shown her these pictures or told her about this young man that was obviously important enough to preserve?"

"She read several entries towards the back of the journal. There she found more pictures, who the young man was, and more importantly, who my father was. Auntie decided to take the pictures and journals home and leave the rest of its contents in the box. Taking them home would give her an opportunity to digest it all."

"Being her nosey self, she learned more than what she had bargained for. Auntie said she knew she had to decide how to break this information to me. She decided to wait until I was settled in college before she told me about the box. She waited my whole freshman year. **A WHOLE year.** Who does that? Didn't tell **NOBODY!** Not even Uncle Barnell. He was kinda bent out of shape too. She said she wanted to tell me many times, but I was studying for exams or involved in some project or another and getting beautiful grades, so she didn't want to break my stride with news like this."

"I still have not read the journals myself. Auntie locked the journals away saying there was really personal stuff in her writings, and I can wait to read them when I'm grown

...

for real. Who knows when that will be? Nobody, not even Aunt Opal."

"Child, I can tell you this, you did not get your sense of humor from your dad. That is a fact. Your father does not have a humorous bone in his body. Pitiful soul...just pit-tee-ful!"

"My mom never told anyone the identity of my birth father, especially after she married. As much as I loved my mother, I was a little upset she withheld information about my birth father from me. To be honest, I guess I never really felt the need to pursue his identity until Auntie found him in the safe deposit box."

"You cannot imagine the shock of learning about the box and about my father, Mr. Timothy Wade Martin of Beaufort, SC. We have been here several times for the Gullah Festival. We were probably standing next to each other and didn't even know it."

"Anyways..."

"Akina, I'm sorry for cutting you off, but he says the same thing."

"What?"

"Anyways...with a 's' on the end like it's two. He has said it like that all his life. Who knows where he picked it up from." Phyllis laughed, *"Probably from his father's side of the family!"*

"Wow, that's funny. I've said it all my life too. I remember once my mom said she had a friend that use to say 'anyways'. Obviously, she never told me who her friend was."

"Anyways", she laughed, "my Auntie wanted to check the Martin family out, especially Wade Martin, to see if they would be safe for me. I guess she felt the last thing I needed in my life was more crazies and more leeches. That's how you met my Auntie because she followed the trail and found you. So by the time I learned about you and my father, my mother had been dead a little over a year.

Phyllis had hardly said a word. She just listened to Akina's story, some of which, Opal Williams had already told her. She remembered Opal saying she did not understand how Rebeca could keep such a secret. When Rebeca realized she was pregnant, she was determined not to discuss the father.

Phyllis took Akina's hands, "Darlin', regardless of how you got here, I am so happy that you are, and we will make many memories from now on. And besides, how cool is it your deciding to come to college nearby. This was no coincidence. God knew exactly what He was doing, and He don't make no mistakes!"

"Grandma, did my Auntie tell you there was an entry that said her biggest regret was losing you?"

Phyllis hugged her granddaughter, happy there will be many, many more hugs to come. After all, this is a first for both of them. Phyliss never had a granddaughter and Akina never had a grandmother. What an adventure this will be for the two of them.

...

Chapter 18
Phyllis's Letter

For Phyllis, it was a lot to take in…an adult granddaughter she did not know about and was pretty sure Wade did not know about. She had prayed continuously Wade would settle down, marry and have children. That never happened and now he is in his late fifties and in prison, suffering with paranoid schizophrenia. For a while, Phyllis knew in her spirit her son was neither morally nor mentally capable of having a substantial relationship and let's not start to talk about the fact that he was now too old to have children. Maybe not physically, but certainly emotionally.

Even in jail, Wade still acts as if he has no family. He barely calls them, and there were times when they have driven the two to three hours to visit him and he refused to even accept visitors, not even his mother. The day she went to tell him about Akina was no exception. Phyllis cried all the way back home. When she returned home, she told her neighbor how devastated she was. "I am his mother. How can he justify refusing to see me when I come to visit him? I am the one that did the best I could to raise him and to shield him from my father, and his stepfather, although he blamed me for everything that happened to him at the hands of his grandfather and his stepfather. I admitted I could have refused to divorce Marcus, and I made the choice to marry again. How was I supposed to know how it would all turn out? And now I have to talk to him about Akina. What am I going to do?"

Phyllis decided to write him a letter. Surely, he will read the letter. Phyllis felt it was important her son knew he had a daughter. She felt maybe, somehow, this realization just might help him to change his lifestyle, take steps to mend his broken spirit and rekindle his relationship with Christ and his family.

The letter read…

"Wade, I pray this letter finds you as well as can be expected, under the circumstances. I'm not sure why you make it so difficult for people to love you. I understand you went through more than any child should have had to go through and I know much of it was my fault for not halting the madness sooner. However, you are grown, and I expected by now you would have realized happiness is not what you have done, but what you can do now. And now, I have news for you that is very important and will cause a great change in both of our lives.

Her name is Phyllis Akina Williams. She is Rebeca Williams, daughter. She is your daughter. Rebeca knew how much I loved her, thus her first name. However, she goes by her middle name, Akina. Rebeca never mentioned to me or you that, when she left for Atlanta and graduate school, she was pregnant. She found out about four months after she left and decided not to tell you. This explains why she stopped communicating with me. I'm sure you remember me asking if you had heard from her and that we never got around to going to look for her.

She lived with her aunt and uncle, in Atlanta, who helped her throughout her pregnancy and helped raise Akina, during and after her college days. Akina said whenever she would ask her about us, Rebeca would give an excuse or just say they will talk about it later. They never got a chance to talk about it later. Rebeca and her husband were killed in a plane crash when Akina was sixteen years old. Akina found me because, Rebeca's diary had information and pictures of us. Rebeca's wishes were that Akina not know about you and the other contents of the box until she was twenty-one. When her aunt realized the identity of her father was in the diary, instead of giving it directly to Akina, she came to visit me.

The diary had a lifetime of entries in it, but the last few chapters was about the time you and she spent together. Days upon days of entries about the good, bad and indifferent of your relationship. As well as the anguish she went through when you all separated, her leaving alone and then founding out she was pregnant, as well as why she chose not to tell you about Akina. Akina felt her mother must had planned to reveal everything to her on her nineteen birthday, when she could make a decision of whether or not she wanted to look for us. In the safe deposit box was keepsakes of your relationship. She found pictures of you and Rebeca, as well as old letters and pictures from me, which is how her aunt found me. She called me, told me who she was and asked if she could visit me.

Wade, I'm sorry you are receiving this news this way, but I came to see you and you refused to see me. You do not call. If you want to know more about your daughter, and yes, she is definitely your daughter, you know you can call me.

With all my love, Mom."

Two weeks later, her postman handed her an envelope with a post office stamp reading, RETURN TO SENDER.

Talking to her neighbor, Phyllis said, "This is the letter I sent him. He never opened it, just sent it back. I am so angry. I don't know what to do. I had to pray for supernatural strength from the Lord, because I want to storm that jail and beat him!" Jesus Himself had to calm me down! Ha! It's funny now, but earlier I could have bit the head off a rattlesnake!"

"So what will you do?" asked her neighbor.

"I will send another letter to the Chaplain of the jail and ask him to give it to Wade's psychologist, or maybe they both could sit him down and make him read it."

Shaking her head and laughing, she said she never thought she would have to take these types of actions with her son.

The following week she received a call from Wade.

Anyone that has been sheltered from the life of an inmate behind bars, jail phone calls only last fifteen minutes. At the end of fifteen minutes, the phone automatically disconnects with no regard for what was being said nor the emotional state of the caller or callee. In the fifteen minutes allotted I explained as much as I could and asked him if I came to visit him would he accept the visit? He said yes.

During her visit, Phyllis told Wade as much as she knew about Rebeca and Akina. She showed him pictures of Akina. He cried the entire visit; however, when she asked him if he wanted to meet Akina, he said no. He did not want her to see him in jail and anything Rebeca told her about their breakup would probably make her hate him. Phyllis reminded him he would be released soon which will give him an opportunity to meet on his terms...outside of the prison.

...

She tried to console her son and assure him that Akina did not hate him and is eager to meet him. No matter what Phyllis said, Wade refused to meet his daughter, 'not now and probably not later.' His words exactly.

"So," *Phyllis said to her neighbor,* "we wait, and we pray."

Chapter 19: *Session 24*
I Have A Daughter?

"I never had good romantic relationships."

"The only resemblance of a relationship I ever had was with Rebeca Williams. I didn't think she would go out with me, but she did. She was ten years younger than me and I loved her because she was a free spirit and obeyed the rules just enough to remain on the dean's honor roll. She was not clingy like other girls. She did not care who my family was or what they had. She was a sophomore in college, studying photography and journalism and her ultimate plan was to travel the world telling stories through her camera. Loving her also caused anxiety for me. I did not want to feel someone else could love me. If my own family didn't love me, why should she."

"So, as much as I loved her, I allowed The Voices to ruin the relationship for me. I liked that she wasn't clingy, but we decided the only way to assure her love and loyalty was to control her every move. I remember when she left for her internship, The Voices made me obsessed with fear and jealousy to the point that when she returned, I was full of doubts about her. We dated throughout her senior year (off and on), but I made it difficult for her. I often think about those days. I knew she loved me, and I knew I needed her,

...

but I don't know why I had to make it so difficult for her. When I was with Rebeca, my spirit was at rest. The Voices would try to interrupt, but it was easier to ignore them when she was around me."

"When she told me she accepted a graduate program in Atlanta, all I could think about was her leaving and forgetting about me. Once I started letting the jealousy in, The Voices would talk louder. It was as if I could not help myself and then I'd be angry, accusing her of things that, in my right mind, I knew were not true. I don't know how she stayed with me as long as she did. I was angry she was leaving. She wanted me to go with her. I remember her saying I can drive trucks from anywhere. I didn't have to stay in South Carolina. I wanted to say yes, however, I had to refuse to move with her because I had to stay close to MMTrucking. The Voices reminded me that if I left, my dad would give everything to Antonio and leave me nothing."

"You know what Doc, right now this minute I can hear them saying, *We did the right thing to get rid of her. She wasn't like us.*'"

As is his habit, he put his hands on his head as if he needed to hold The Voices inside.

"You know what I think? I think The Voices were always worried about Rebeca, especially The Evil One. They know she was good for me and if I stayed with her, that would be the end of them."

"So, she left, and I stayed. I did not tell her about the voices. Rebeca did not know she was pregnant and when she realized she was, she chose not to tell me about the baby. It doesn't surprise me she didn't tell me. I came from dysfunction and she came from dysfunction. She was the youngest of her birth parent's children; however, they were not a part of her life at all. Her siblings and other relatives were all dysfunctional and not in a position to care for her. She grew up in Atlanta with her father's twin brother and his wife, Barnell and Opal Williams. WOW! How is it I still remember their names? She showed me pictures of their house. It was a large house, so it worked out perfectly for them to raise Rebeca, and subsequently, I guess, her... well... our daughter, Akina. My mother said despite her pregnancy, she completed her master's degree in commercial photography. I didn't realize how close she and my mom were. She loved and missed her enough to name her daughter Phyllis Akina, but she never told us about her... because of me. Her Aunt Opal called her Akina and everyone agreed. According to my mother, Rebeca planned to tell Akina about me and our family, she just never got around to it."

"Wade, was there ever an opportunity for you to try to find Rebeca?"

...

After a long sigh, Wade slowly nodded his head, "Yes, I knew how to find her people and some years ago, I saw some of her work in a magazine. I knew it was her even before I saw her picture. She was still so beautiful. Then, I noticed her last name had changed. Hyphen-something. She was married. My heart hurt and The Voices started laughing. The article said her family lived in New York, and I assumed children belonged to him and her. Not me. I remember how sad I was to have thrown us away the way I did. Now she is dead, and I never got a chance to tell her what was really going on and how much I needed her in my life."

"Did I ever tell you that, other than Abuelita, she was the only person that could make me feel safe when The Voices were yelling? When my Abuelita died, I was lost, and The Voices were relentless. Remember I told you I didn't tell anyone except my grandmother about the voices? Well, that wasn't actually true. I told Abuelita and she never told anyone. And Rebeca heard me yelling at them. When she asked me about it I told her it was a nightmare. That happened a couple times. I should have known then she didn't care about The Voices because she loved me. I let them convince me she would make fun of me and desert me, just like the others."

Wade sat in his spot, under the window, in silence, until it was time to return to his cell.

...

Chapter 20: Session 25
I Didn't Know Because I Didn't Care

Wade came to see me right after visiting hours were over. He did not have an appointment.

"Hello Wade, how have you been?"

"A little better than worse."

"I'm sure you are still processing the fact that you have an adult daughter."

"And to make matters worse, now I know why my brother has not come to look for me…and, once again, it's all my fault.

"I don't understand…what do you mean 'it's all your fault." What is all your fault?"

"Once or twice, I wondered if Antonio would ever come back to see me. The last time he visited me, I was less than stellar. The Voices would tell me not to worry about the half-and-half. The Evil One kept saying he won't be a problem for much longer but wouldn't tell me what that meant and after a while, I didn't worry about it."

"All these conversations you forced me to have with you has made me start to question my actions in the past, and how I had been a disappointment to my father and how I mistreated my brother, including the last time he was here."

...

"Glad to be of service. Isn't that a good thing...you're beginning to relate your actions to the consequences you have had to live with?"

"Maybe, but The Voices have been louder lately than ever. Since my mom told me about my daughter, I've tried to ignore them, shut them out, which was something I did not always do before. Even with Nurse Johnson's medication, they will not stop talking."

And then today, my sister, Esabelle, came to see me. I was happy to see her. She brought me up to date on family news. Someone is having a baby. Someone is getting married, that sort of thing. I told her I understood why Antonio hadn't been to see me for a while. I was very belligerent towards him the last time he came. The next thing she said rocked me to my soul.

At this moment, I see tears welling up in Wade's eyes.

"She told me Antonio had not visited me because he is very sick. She said Antonio had a stroke and that's when they all, including Lizanne, found out he had prostate cancer. He never told anyone. He didn't want to bother us, with everything else that was going on. Which is a polite way of saying with me f... (shaking his head) messing up everything!"

"I started crying, which none of the family had ever seen before. Esabelle tried to assure me Antonio would be

...

alright, and he would visit as soon as he was strong enough to travel."

"Doc, at that moment, I understood what The Voices meant when they said he won't be a problem for long. They meant that he was going to die!"

Again Wade is at the window, rubbing his head...

"Even though I was afraid to know the answer, I asked her on what day did he have the stroke. When she told me, I knew then I had almost killed my brother. First, Marguerite, then my dad, now my brother. I'm a murderer! I told her it was my fault Antonio was sick; because I treated him so badly, just like it was my fault our father got sick. I kept telling her I tried to be good. The Voices helped me stay angry, so I didn't really try to ignore them and now my brother will die because of me."

"Esabelle just kept saying everyone was fine and looking forward to Antonio getting better and coming home; and, they were looking forward to me coming home. I asked her how that could be when I tried to ruin everything and kill my brother. She just kept saying if Jesus could forgive the people that crucified Him, then I must rest easy knowing the ENTIRE family has already forgiven me for what I did."

Wade sat on the floor, holding his head, constantly telling The Voices to be quiet and repeating, **"I already know! You..."** *He stopped short of continuing the statement.*

...

"Wade, you already know what? What are The Voices telling you?"

"Doc, all my life, I wanted to be good. I tried to ignore the 'voices,' but it was too hard. The 'voices' helped me stay angry at everyone and everything. Anger turned my brother away. Anger turned my mother away. Anger turned Rebeca away. Now, Rebeca is dead, my dad is dead, Marguerite is dead, and my brother will die because of me. Don't you see, I'm a murderer. The Evil One told me I was a murderer...*and he is right*. I am a murderer...I never wanted to be a murderer...I hurt all over...it's too hard."

"Wade, who is the Evil One? Whose voice is it"

"I **already told you** I will die if I say his name out loud! I have to go now. I won't see you anymore...I won't be back. It's too hard."

As he banged on the door for the guard, he looks at me with an eerie calmness that I had not seen in him before. However, I have seen that look before...

"Wade, come see me tomorrow morning after breakfast. I will tell the morning guard to bring you."

"Sure, we'll see..."

*"**Promise me Wade!** Promise you will come here immediately after breakfast! Do you understand!"*

Wade a little startled at her tone. It was a tone of urgency he had not heard from her before. Frowning, he agreed with her, "Yeah, okay…tomorrow."

As soon as he was gone, I called the ward and the night psychiatrist to place a guard to watch him for the rest of the day and that Officer Jonathan Pierce be the guard to watch him all night.

Even though I had other clients that day, I struggled, concerned that Wade's spirit was not in a good place.

Chapter 21
They Would Be Better Off…

Wade paced…back and forth…from wall to wall in his room…talking out loud…

"My brain hurts…hurts…hurts, even in prison, you keep bothering me…still haunting me, day in and day out! And now Doc keeps bothering me about who you are. Why does *she* need to know ya'lls name? I **told** her I will die if I call your name. Obviously, *she* wants me to die!"

"First, my mother tells me I have a daughter and that Rebeca is dead. I could have heard anything else but that. Rebeca has been tormenting me for months. Now I know why…she's dead. So now will she become a voice in my head, probably hostile too? I was so selfish towards her. Was she really so angry with me that she couldn't tell me we had made a daughter together? She hated me and I'm sure my daughter has learned all about me and all of the horrible things I've done and hates me too. How can I face her? How can she be happy knowing her father is a schizophrenic, maniac convict murderer?"

And if that wasn't enough, Esabelle tells me Antonio almost died on the same day I cursed him out and told him I never needed to see him again!

"*Why* am I even here. I am a menace to everyone I come in contact with. What use am I to anybody? Everyone would have been better off if I had died in that alley or when I had that overdose, or better yet, when my grandfather wanted to have me aborted. What kind of second chance has my life been."

Some Jesus people brought magazines for everyone. Wade threw it in the corner and forgot about it. It was supposed to go into the trash, but it never made it.

Bending down to pick it up, "What…I thought I threw this in the trash…not in the mood for Jesus right now!"

As he was about to throw it in the bin, Wade wondered why he was noticing it now. It was almost glowing in his hand. On the cover was a picture of Jesus embracing a man as he cried and the caption said, "Jesus paid it all, even for me."
The Voices started screaming so loud.

"DON'T LOOK AT IT! DON'T READ IT! PICK UP THE GLASS! USE THE GLASS NOW! RELEASE THE PAIN!"

When The Voices took a breath, Wade could hear his dad's voice just as if he were standing in the room. *"Satan's plan is to steal your joy, kill your spirit and destroy your chances of salvation. Satan plans to kill you in your sin. If you die in your sin, your soul will be forever lost."*

Wade sat on the floor leaning against the bed with the magazine in one hand and the piece of glass he found in the courtyard in the other hand.

…

Unaware of how long he sat there staring at the magazine cover, staring at the glass and listening to The Voices scream at him, again he could hear his father's voice, "Satan's plan is to steal your joy, kill your spirit and destroy your chances of salvation."

Wade looked up at the ceiling and yelled at God...

"You were NEVER there for me, EVER!"

"Why should I trust You now?"

"Why should I believe in You now?"

"Give me one reason!"

"When I open this magazine the answer better be on the first page I see, or it will be all over for You!"

"DO YOU HEAR ME GOD?!!"

Almost in a whisper and sobbing, "All over for You!"

Wade held the magazine up, flicking the pages with his finger, then dropped it on the floor. Then The Voices came back even louder!

"DON'T LOOK AT IT! DON'T READ IT! PICK UP THE GLASS! USE THE GLASS NOW!"

The Evil One screamed, **"Release us and you from the pain! Stop the noise forever. Just DO IT! PUT US ALL OUT OF OUR MISERY!"**

On the page in a caption box it said, *"Create in me a clean heart, O God; and renew a right spirit within me."* (Psalms 51:10 KJV)

Wade opened his mouth to talk and The Evil One started screaming again… **"You know He don't care about you! He don't care if you die right now!"**

"If He cared about you, He would not have let it happen to you!"

"You sinned against heaven and against God. Just like me, you are not worthy to be called His son!" Luke 15:21 (NIV)

Wade, holding the glass, looking at the magazine, **"BE QUIET! BE QUIET! I TOLD YOU NEVER TO TALK ABOUT THAT AGAIN! I won't talk about it EVER! SHUT UP!"**

Wade w*himpering,* **"I will kill you first."**

The guard looked in the window of Wade's door to see what he was doing. Wade was pacing the floor with the book in one hand and the glass in the other. The guard did not see the glass.

The Evil One laughed loud and with a sneering, cynical voice, he said, **"Very well. Ha! I don't mind dying, again, what about you Wade? Are you ready to die today?!"**

Wade yelled back at The Evil One, **"JUST SHUT UP! I hate you! I've hated you all my life! All of this is YOUR FAULT…Your fault…my fault!"**

Wade didn't realize he was yelling at the top of his lungs until the guard banged on his cell door and told him to keep it down! The Evil One laughed and said, *'I guess they don't care if something might really be wrong with you!'*

The Evil One was wrong. The guard did know something was wrong because Dr. Stewart informed the staff that he is on suicide watch.

Wade could hear The Voices telling him to cut his wrist, just get it over with! Still holding the piece of glass, he looked at the magazine. A box on the other page caught his eye. He read aloud, *"Come to me, all you who are weary and burdened, and I will give you rest." Matthew 11:28 (NIV).*

When The Voices heard him reading the verse out loud, they started screaming, **"No! NO! It's not true. He won't help you! The only way to get rest is to sleep while the blood flows…LET THE BLOOD FLOW NOW!!!"**

As Wade pressed the glass down on his vein, all he could hear was the loud voices yelling and urging him to let the blood flow. At the sight of the first drops of blood, somehow through all of the noise, Wade could hear Abuelita's soft voice…

"Pequeno…reza" (Little One…pray).

...

173

Wade told her he didn't know how. Again he heard Abuelita say...

"Pequeno...reza" (Little One...pray). "Pídele que los detenga. Pídele que los haga desaparecer." (Ask Him to stop them. Ask Him to make them go away.) "

Wade cried, "God, make them shut up... PLEASE...make them go away!"

And they laughed, ***"We are not afraid of Him. He can't make us lea..."***

Wade just stared at the glass and the magazine. "God, please. You said if I ask in your name...I am so tired...I'm burdened down with all of the bad things I've done...I've hurt too many people. The Evil One is right, why would You care about me after everything I've done..."

He didn't realize his voice was the only voice he was hearing. At first he wasn't sure if they were gone. He just sat there in complete silence. Finally, he heard another familiar voice from his childhood say, "The *Loud Voices are gone Wade. Only your Abuelita, the one you call The Evil One and the ones you call The Whisperers remain. The Evil One is quiet for now. You are fine. Everything will be different for you, if you choose to be with Me, because I still choose to be with you."*

Tears streamed down his face. It had been a long time since he had quiet in his head. Not since Rebeca.

...
174

The guard outside his door realized it was suddenly quiet and felt a slow rise of panic as he knocked on the door while fumbling for the correct key to Wade's room. Wade heard the keys but couldn't move. When the guard opened the door, he told him he was fine. The guard asked him about all of the yelling.

"Nightmares…"

"Really," the guard said, as if accepting Wade's excuse while he picked up the glass, closed the door and resumed his position outside of his door. Wade wanted to panic, but he was too tired. He looked down at his wrist and realized he was bleeding. He tore a T-Shirt and wrapped his arm.

In the quiet, Wade heard The Whisperers. He had not heard them for a very long time. He thought The Evil One had killed them.

"Wade, it is time. You won't die. We will help you if you let us."

"I can't…"

"You must…"

"I will die…"

"No, you won't. We will help you. We will take care of you…"

"How…he is too strong…too mean."

"Trust us….trust Him."

Wade stared at the picture of a man weak and exhausted, falling into the arms of Jesus.

"Why would He care about me. I had not done anything for him to be proud of."

…

"He does care for you. He heard you."

"Why?..."

"...But while he was still a long way off, his father saw him and was filled with compassion for him...threw His arms around him and kissed him." Luke 15:2 (NIV).

...

CHAPTER 22
And The Moral Of The Message Is...?

When the morning alarms started, Wade woke up, still on the floor, still in his clothes from the day before, still in his cell and a little groggy as to what exactly happened to him. Obviously, he wasn't out partying all night, or drinking or getting high. Once his brain cleared, and he noticed his arm, he started to remember the episode from the night before. He wasn't sure what was reality and what was a nightmare. Then he remembered praying. He figured the praying was part of the nightmare because he did not remember the last time he prayed on purpose. However, the real question in his mind was, "Did I *really* hear Jesus talking to me...or...was this a new voice joining the bunch to become another menace in my mind?"

Then, he realized something very unfamiliar to him, something he had not heard in many, many years. Silence. Now there was noise all around him. In the corridor outside of his cell, the bells were ringing to go from here to there and people were talking to each other outside his cell. In the midst of all the noise, he realized it was quiet. There was silence in his head. The continuous buzz that had become a normal part of his existence was gone. The chattering when he was trying to think, was gone. The demands for his attention…gone. The screaming when he told them to be quiet…silent. The voices that plagued him the majority of his life were quiet. He knew they were not just sleeping, because a couple of them snore, loudly, and he did not hear snoring. He was trying to comprehend how it happened, how they were for real quiet! He walked around his cell, trying to remember what happened the night before, trying to figure out what happened to The Voices.

The last time he had this feeling of peace was when he stood next to his father in Puerto Rico at his wedding to Marguerite.

As he paced the floor, he stepped on the magazine. The entire scene returned, and he remembered the screaming, the glass, his dad, Jesus and Abuelita, the quiet and The Whisperers. He sat on his bed, with his head in his hands trying to hold back tears.

He read the text over and over and asked God to forgive him and help him to have a clean heart and a right spirit.

The officer opened his door to tell him Dr. Stewart wanted to see him. He thought to himself, "Wow, what a story for Doc. This story will blow her mind."

...

Chapter 23: *Session 26*
Never Forsake You…

When Wade walked into Dr. Stewart's office, the first thing he saw was the piece of glass on the table.

"I…"

Before he could finish his statement, she held up her hand and motioned for him to have a seat. She stood in front of his window, not talking…not wanting him to see how upset she was; and Wade sat on the couch, squirming, wondering when the guards would come to lock him in the secure side of the psych ward, where the suicide risks are. Just the thought made him tremble because, people die up there.

"Wade, yesterday when you said you may not see me again, I asked you to come see me this morning after breakfast…am I correct?"

"Yes." *his tone sarcastic* "Actually, I said I don't know."

"And then did I not ask you to promise me you would come this morning?"

"I said sure"

"And did I ask you if you understood what I was asking you? Did you say yes, and did you promise me?"

Rubbing his head sounding a little irritated and sorrowful, "Yes and Yes."

"So, what happened? Because, it seems as if you were considering suicide last night, which, would have prevented you from coming to see me this morning."

...

She turned to face him, "Wade, were you considering suicide last night?"

He didn't want to answer that question. He rubbed his wrist, now covered with a long sleeve shirt. He didn't want to think about how close he came, again, to ending his life.

"Yes."

Then with a sarcastic tone he asked, "Anyways, if you believed I promised, why did you put a guard outside my door?"

"Because I have been in this business for a long time, I recognize the signs. You said you promised in order to appease me, not, because you meant it. Hence, your sore wrist that you are hiding under that long sleeve shirt. And, so, I gave instructions for someone to watch you the rest of the day. And, because I pray, the God you hate, and who you think hates you, told me to request a specific guard as your night watch."

Wade scrunched his face and primped his lips to keep from saying the words trying to find a way out of his mouth...

"Nobody asked you to do all that! Why would God care about me anyways?"

"He cares for you Wade. So much so the guard He said to put outside your door wasn't supposed to work last night. He was called in because another guard did not come in."

(agitated) "What has that to do with me Doc?"

Dr. Stewart sits down and looks directly into Wade's eyes...

...

"He, the guard, knows who you are. He has watched you before. He remembers you from high school. He said you tutored him in math. He is a Christian and he told me he prayed for you all night. During your outbursts of yelling with The Voices, the guard prayed for you. While you were yelling at God, he continued to pray. He called me and told me how your night went."

Holding up the glass, she continued, "and, he brought me this."

Wade would not look at her, but just held his head in his hands.

Not knowing The Voices were gone she wondered what they were saying to him at that moment, but instead, she asked him, "So what happened?"

So Wade told her what happened. He told her The Evil One told him everyone hated him, including God, and he should just end it all. He told her about the magazine, about him yelling at God and The Voices yelling at him to use the glass...to let the blood flow, so the pain would go away. He told her about hearing a conversation his dad had with him about Satan wanting to destroy him and about Abuela, telling him to pray. And, about when he did, The Voices stopped yelling. He told her about how Jesus talked to him in the voice he remembered as a child and told him the loud voices were gone, except for The Evil One, who was quiet for now. He told her how The Whisperers told him he would not die... then he stopped talking.

After a moment, Dr. Stewart broke the silence...

"What did they mean. 'you would not die'?"

Wade stood and walked to the window and almost in a whisper, "If I say who The Evil One is..."

...

"So are you ready to say who The Evil One is?"

Wade was again silent for a long moment.

"So…do you think I should let my daughter come to visit me here. My mom thinks I should, but I don't want her to meet me for the first time in this get up *(pointing to his clothes)*. What do you think, Doc?"

"It's up to you Wade. Your mother did say your daughter wants to meet you, right? And I'm sure your mother did not tell her EVERYTHING about you. That, will be your job, if you want her to know who you are…and are not."

"Hmmm," *Wade pondered what she said, however, he did not respond.*

"However, you cannot avoid the truth forever. Until you identify who The Evil One is and why you call him The Evil One, you will never completely heal, and you will never be safe from whatever it is that he represents."

Tearfully, "Maybe, but I'm afraid. The Whisperers said they will help me, but I'm afraid he will kill them too!"

"Do you know who Nelson Mandela was? Do you know his life struggle?"

"Yes, of course!"

I want you to read this to me, out loud."

A little irritated, Wade responded, **"What…Why?!"**

"Because I asked you to…read it please…"

Still irritated Wade reads, "I learned that courage was not the absence of fear, but the triumph over it." *Sneering over his glasses he continued,* "The brave man is not he who does not feel afraid, but he who conquers that fear." — **Nelson Mandela**

"Wade as long as you allow the fear of The Evil One to control you, you will never be able to manage a true relationship with yourself, with anyone else nor with God. The only constant in your life will always be The Evil One. Right now, you hold the cards, but he is still in control of the game."

"Dr. Stewart, sometimes I really don't like you and there are times when you really get on my nerves, but I am sorry I allowed the fear to dictate what I did and almost did last night. I'm sorry I forgot I promised you."

"I understand and I appreciate the apology."

As he was leaving the office, Wade stood in the window, watching the men play basketball. Again he wished he had friends to hang out with, to come see about him, to care if he was dead or alive. He wondered if his family would ever forgive him for everything he had done. He wondered if Rebeca ever forgave him. He wondered if his daughter really wanted a relationship with him, or, if she wanted to see this terrible man that her mother chose to erase out of their lives.

"Doc, would you call my mom and ask her to come to see me? Will she be allowed to see me in your office? Will you come with her?"

"I can make that happen."

...

"Good. Just send for me when she is here."

"Have a good day Doc…and I am sorry…it's just…"

"I understand Wade. Have a good night. We'll talk tomorrow."

Chapter 24
Evil Becomes Good…

"It is that you planned to do something bad to me. But really, God was planning good things. God's plan was to use me to save the lives of many people. And that is what happened."
Genesis 50:20 (ERV)

Antonio visited Wade once or twice a month after he was released to travel by his doctor. Someone had to drive him for the first few visits. Once his doctor released him to drive, he went alone. Lizanne was not happy with him driving two and a half hours alone. Sometimes she would ride with him and spend her time away from the prison while he visited with Wade.

Although it's been two years, she still had no real desire to see Wade. Lizanne knew eventually she would have to make peace with him and her anger towards him. He caused havoc, not only in his family, but in hers as well. He intended to pull her brother into his mess and he almost killed her husband. She really prayed and prayed for help so she would be able to be around him in peace when he returns home, which will be soon. Lizanne wondered what the Martin Family Thanksgiving Gathering would be like with Wade there, if he even came. She only remembers him coming once before their dad passed away. Since he has been

...

locked up, their lives have been peaceful. Antonio has mended well. He is still under maintenance care with his doctors, but he is doing well. The family has increased by two and a half – one birth, one marriage with a birth soon to come. MMTrucking is back on track and running smoothly, while continuing to replace the clients lost because of the scandal Wade caused. Ironically, Antonio was able to pick-up several of McIntosh Trucking clients and provide jobs for many more people.

McIntosh Trucking was under federal legal actions as a result of various illegal and fraudulent activities conducted by its owner, Joseph McIntosh. After the part McIntosh played in Wade's attempt to crush MMTrucking and Antonio's reputation, McIntosh Trucking was ordered to cease all operations until the investigation was completed. McIntosh Trucking's misfortune became MMTrucking saving grace.

They tried to harm MMTrucking, but God turned their evil into good allowing MMTrucking to flourish.

On one of their visit's Wade asked Antonio, again, to forgive him for everything he did – ever. They talked about the voices. The Whisperers, Abuelita, his grandmother, their Dad and The Loud Voices. He told him what happened the night he thought about committing suicide. He told him about the magazine. He told him about The Evil One who

...

taunts him day and night and how he told him he could make everyone happy by just letting his blood flow. Wade told Antonio about their dad reminding him Satan wanted to kill him in his sins. He told him in the midst of The Voices yelling and screaming he heard Abuelita telling him to pray and when he did The Loud Voices stopped and Jesus told him they were gone.

There were so many questions Antonio wanted to ask. He was afraid if he interrupted, Wade would stop talking. So, he chose to hold his questions for later.

Wade told Antonio about Dr. Stewart and how she keeps saying he has to say who The Evil One is…call his name. He told him how, she kept saying that if he didn't, he would never heal or have a decent relationship with anyone and that The Evil One would never go away. He told him how he was afraid because a long time ago, when he was alive, The Evil One told him if he ever told he would die.

He had tears welling up in his eyes and he tried hard not to cry in front of his little brother. Antonio had tears too, because he could sense the pain and anguish of his brother. So, they both sat in silence for a few minutes.

Then, Antonio asked him if someone hurt him and is that someone now the voice of The Evil One. Wade laughed and told him he sounded like Doc. Wade was not ready to answer that question to Antonio. His mom was coming the next day and he had to tell her first.

Just then, he felt a sharp pain in his head, as if someone was sticking hot needles in his brain. When Antonio asked him what was wrong, Wade said he had a headache all day and it must be turning into a migraine. He will go to the nurse and get something for the pain.

Since visiting hours were almost over, Wade shocked Antonio by asking him to pray for him before he left. Antonio prayed, hugged his brother, and left.

Antonio continued to pray for his brother because, in his spirit, he felt Wade's headache was a little more than he let on and that somehow The Evil One had something to do with it.

That night The Evil One got his voice back. Wade couldn't get to sleep. The Evil One continued with his rants, taunts, accusation and threats that if he told anyone his name, he would die.

Finally, Wade heard The Whisperers tell him they will be with him when the time comes. Then he heard Abuelita. She told him to pray…Jesus will protect him. Then, he fell into a sound sleep and, The Evil One was quiet, again.

...

Chapter 25: *Session 27*
What Is His Name…

Early in the morning, The Evil One woke Wade to warn him that he meant what he said all those years ago. He told Wade he would kill him if he told anyone…EVER. Wade wondered what Dr. Stewart said to his mom. He hoped she didn't say too much just in case he chickened out.

Before the guard came to escort him, he looked at the picture on the now tattered magazine. He reminded God that his father and Abuelita told him He would be with him during his time of trouble. Now is his time of trouble.

He looked in the mirror. New haircut, trimmed bread and mustache. He was ready to see his mom and if he died today, well, at least he looked good.

When Wade walked into Dr. Stewart's office, his mom was not there. With a little attitude in his voice, Wade said, "I thought you said my mother would be here."

"Good morning, Wade. How are you? Oh me, I'm fine thanks for asking!"

"Your mother is here, just not in here. I wanted a few minutes with you before she joined us."

Wade hung his head a little, "Oh, I'm sorry and I'm okay, as well as can be expected, especially with him reminding me I'm on death row and all."

"Oh, The Evil One? When did he wake up?"

"Yesterday when Antonio came to visit. I think he gave me a migraine when I told Antonio I would tell him later about the threats."

"What do you mean he "gave you a migraine?" The voices have never caused you to feel pain before, have they?"

"No, this was the first time. I still have a headache…like needles stabbing my brain!"

"What part of your brain? Show me."

Wade put his hands on his forehead and the top of his head.

"Here."

"Your frontal lobe, the area around your forehead, house your emotions, cognitive or thought processes, your ability to reason and decipher right from wrong, etc. Your emotions and thought processes are in overdrive and you are preparing to do something that will be life-changing, for you and The Evil One."

"Possibly life-ending…"

"No, if you are positive, the outcome will always be positive. If you are negative…well, I'm sure you understand. It's up to you."

"The Whisperers said they will help me. Abuelita said to pray and that Jesus will protect me. So, I'll just have to have faith…right? Something I have not practiced in a while, at least not in Him."

Wade sat in his usual chair and began to rub his head as he does when there is too much chatter in his brain.

When he saw his mother, he hugged her and hugged her and hugged her, as if he may never get another chance. He is so much taller

…

and larger than her, that when he wrapped his arms around her, she almost disappeared. He asked her, over and over to forgive him for causing her so much pain. His mother did what most mother's do. She rubbed his back and told him all was well between them. When he settled down, she asked him if this was why he sent for her. She told him how excited she was that he would be home soon and that she hoped he was ready for Thanksgiving, home cooking — turkey, yams, macaroni pie, sweet potato pie, etc., etc., etc.," He just shook his head and smiled.

Dr. Stewart asked, "Can I come by the day after for left-overs?"

They all laughed, and it sort of calmed the mood some.

Phyllis told Wade how Akina was doing and that she is anxious to meet him. She smiled and touched her son's face, "She favors you."

"Really?" Wade smiled. "Poor child. She must have had a rough life being teased all the time."

Wade's expression faded, "Mom. There's a reason why I asked Doc to bring you here, in her office, instead of in the visitors' room. I have something very important I need to talk to you about, now. Waiting until I got home would not be a good idea because I'm sure I would not say anything. It would remain a deep dark secret that's killing me." *To himself he said, "Why did I say that… now I have to tell her everything. Dangit! Hmmmm…maybe I can make up something…not really."*

Phyllis, looking between her son and Dr. Stewart, "Wade, baby, what is wrong? What are you talking about…are you sick…oh my God! What…"

...

"Mom, it's nothing like that, unless you meant sick in the head." *He laughed, but Phyllis was not amused.*

Dr. Stewart thought she should put Phyllis at ease, at least a little bit. "Mrs. Martin, as you know, Wade suffers with schizophrenia and we have been working on what happened or didn't happen, searching for the root cause of his illness. With God's help, Wade has been able to pray away most of the voices. I'm not sure how much you know about the cause, symptoms and effects of this disease but..."

"I'm sorry," *Phyllis interrupted Dr. Stewart,* "When he prayed? Wade...when you prayed? As far as I know, you have not prayed, since you were young."

"When it was discovered that you were diagnosed with schizophrenia, I was numb for a moment. Then I started researching to learn as much as I could. As I studied, I began to recognize some instances when his actions or reactions mirrored the symptoms. I know hearing voices is a part of it. I was terrified when I learned it could be hereditary, because after he died, my mother told me my father was schizophrenic. If I had known, I may have been more proactive with your health." *Phyllis' voice was low and shaky as she tried to figure out the reason for this visit.* "Wade, why did you ask me to come here? What is it that you couldn't tell me alone or later?"

So, even though his head was pounding and The Evil One was threatening him, Wade began to tell his mother his story.

...

Chapter 26: *Session 28*
His Name Is NOT Wonderful…

Wade felt the anxiety of a teenager about to tell his mom his darkest secret…which, in fact, was about to happen…

"I'm sure you both might have questions, but I don't know if I can say what I have to say and answer questions too. Right now, there are needles in my brain and The Evil One is moaning in my head."

"The Evil One?" Phyllis asked.

"That is the name of the worst of the voices that plaques your son's mind." Dr. Stewart answered Phyllis so Wade wouldn't have to.

"I have been having anxiety for most of my life. I wanted to believe I was just mad at you, dad, Grandfather, your husband and Grandmother…well, everyone. I eventually figured out something was wrong. I started noticing my thoughts were all over the place and I really didn't want to be around or be bothered with anyone because the noise was too loud. When I mentioned it to you and your parents, y'all chalked it up to teenage puberty issues."

"At first it was only The Whisperers. When I tried to kill your husband for beating you and killing my sister, I heard a mean voice I had not heard before. The Whisperers talked me out of it and the mean voice went away."

"After that, I would hear them off and on. I call them The Whisperers because their voices were always quiet and calming, even when they were upset."

"Grandfather would always say I was the cause of everyone's pain, and I believed him. So, I walked around feeling sad and sorry and I let people treat me any kind of way because, after all, I deserved it. After a while, the pain was too much and I just wanted some peace. When I wanted to die, The Whisperers wouldn't let me. They kept telling me to hold on a little while longer and that soon everything would be alright. Ha! They have been telling me that for a long time!"

Wade paused, walked around the room as he usually does when he is searching for words. When he sat down, Phyllis wanted to reach out to him, but she didn't.

"When Dad asked me if I wanted to go with them to California for three years, at first, I thought like, 'hell no' and The Whisperers were yelling YES! GO! … YES! GO! … YES! GO! So, I said yes, because I really did want to go and leave the misery behind. I was so afraid you would let grandfather make you say no. I'm so glad you didn't. I have not had very many seasons of peace nor happiness in my life. California was one of those seasons. My spirit was at peace for three whole years and The Whisperers were quiet pretty much the entire time. I didn't really think about what had happened to me."

"When we came back from California, do you remember how I begged to live with my dad?"

Phyllis responded almost in a whisper, *"Yes."*

"Well, there was a reason, other than the fact I had made peace with him and my bratty brother, something I had never told anyone! Only The Whisperers knew, because they were there when it happened."

Wade rubbed his head with his hands the way he does when he is searching for words through the noise of The Voices. Dr. Stewart wondered if the others were in his head again. When Phyllis positioned herself, again, to touch Wade, Dr. Stewart stopped her. It was not the time to touch him. Phyllis's mind was searching for what he was trying to tell her. What happened to him? And why didn't he feel comfortable telling her?

"You might not remember, when I first came back, you wanted to go shopping and hang out like we used to. We had a great time until I saw Coach with his family. We were laughing about something when I saw him. I guess the look on my face made you turn to see what I saw. It seemed as if he saw me at the same time. I didn't know if I wanted to run and punch him in the face or run in the opposite direction. What do you call that, Doc...fight or flight? In the end I sat there and tried to ignore the fact that he was staring at me and headed to our table."

Wade stands up and begins to pace the floor again. Back and forth…back and forth. He almost seemed to have forgotten others were in the room.

Dr. Stewart asked Wade if he needed a break or needed water. He said no.

In a very sarcastic voice Wade said, "Good afternoon Mrs. Martin, how are you? This is my wife, Mildred and my sons. I haven't seen you and Wade in a very long time. Wade, how have you been? When did you return?"

Phyllis turned to Dr. Stewart and in almost a whisper she said, "I remember that day and the conversation. Wade seemed to panic when his old basketball coach came to the table. Afterwards, I asked him what was wrong. He just wanted to leave. I remember that day."

Wade continued by answering her question, "I was not prepared to see him again, ever. When I did, I panicked, and he knew it."

Again, with a sarcastic tone in his voice, Wade continued his story…

"Wade, it's great to see you back. The team will be happy to see you again. This season's practice begins next week."

Phyllis again speaks towards Dr. Stewart. "I remember thanking the coach and I remember Wade never looking him in the face. I just chalked it up as teenage rudeness and I did fuss at him when the coach walked away. I remember Wade saying he was glad to get off the

...

team and he did not want to go back, and he didn't want to go back to that school. He wanted to go to school in Beaufort and live with his dad. I remember dismissing the entire conversation by saying he would be better off finishing high school with his friends. The truth is, I didn't want him so far away from me again."

"Wade," Dr. Stewart asked, "Why didn't you want to rejoin your team or go back to the school?"

A little agitated, Wade sneered, "What difference does it make. The point is, I did go back to that school because I couldn't live with my dad. I refused to rejoin the Community Center team. Some of the team members started bullying me, saying I became a fa…, I mean, gay while I was in California. The bullying went on for a while. I didn't tell anyone, and it just made me hate God even more. I already hated Him for what he allowed to happen. But now it was starting all over again, as if I had never left."

"Wade, are you telling me the reason you wanted to live with your dad in California and then in Beaufort is because you were being bullied at school?" Phyllis, in tears, continued, "Why didn't you tell someone? Why didn't you tell me or your dad?"

Wade turned to look at his mother. "I did, I told your father, and he laughed and told me to man up! I told him the coach allowed them to bully me, but he didn't care."

"Wade, what do you mean the coach 'allowed' them to bully you?" asked Dr. Stewart.

...

"They were his favorites. It was four of them. The same ones from middle school at the Community Center. When I returned from California, we were all in high school, and he was still the coach."

Wade rubbed his head, "My head is killing me," as he looked at Dr. Stewart, "I told you what he said."

Dr. Stewart and Phyllis looked at each other. Dr. Stewart is very concerned about Wade's emotional stability at this point.

"Wade, we have been here for a while and it might be a good idea if we take a break, if you take a break..."

"I guess a bathroom and water break might be in order, but if I leave this office, I'm not coming back and I'm not putting myself through this again. I'm sure this is difficult for you and mom. It's very difficult for me, trying to say this out loud. "UGH!" *Wade primped his lips to keep from cursing,* "...my head is **killing me**."

Dr. Stewart had lunch brought in and the nurse to bring something for Wade's headache.

Phyllis is sitting, trying to make sense of what she is hearing.

She looked towards Dr. Stewart, "I guess you knew all of this he is talking about?"

"No, he has always refused to tell me, until now."

"Mom, nobody alive knows."

He decided not to tell her that her father knew but refused to do anything about it.

...
198

Wade begins again…

"He allowed them to bully me because he wanted to make sure I stayed afraid. In middle school, he told me if I ever said anything to anyone, he would kill me. And then the bullying started. I was glad to be in California because they couldn't bother me there. I thought after three years, it would have been over, but no. When I saw the coach in the mall, I knew it would just start all over again, if I stayed."

"I should have told you why I wanted to go to Beaufort, but if I told you about the bullying, I would have to tell you why they were bullying me and why they called me a fa…*again Wade primped his lips and sighed…* you know."

Neither Phyllis nor Dr. Stewart had hardly eaten anything from their plates. Phyllis felt almost nauseous trying to anticipate what Wade might say next.

"When I was playing basketball at the community center, Coach helped all of us with our homework. He would answer questions we had because most of us did not have a father in the home, so he sort of took on that role for us. He would take us to ball games at other schools, even colleges. He would buy us things our parents couldn't, like cleats and gloves, stuff like that."

"The problem started when he gave those boys the authority to 'keep us in line'. They could get rough sometimes and sometimes coach would say something to them, but most of the time he didn't. One afternoon, one of the boys was

...

hurt pretty bad. He told his parents it was an accident. He never came back."

"It didn't take long to realize the relationship between coach and these boys was different."

Wade went to the window rubbing his head and looked out on the courtyard. He was quiet for a while.

He took a deep breath as if it was hard for him to breathe normally. Almost in a whisper,

"They attacked me in the shower…"

Almost simultaneously, both Doc and Phyllis asked, "They?"

"The boys." *Wade continued staring out of the window.* "It was four of them. They were naked. They started playing with each other. I hope y'all know what that means because I really don't want to have to spell it out. Anyways, they were playing with each other and when I tried to leave, they pushed me back in the shower."

Wade was struggling to hold back tears and keep a voice clear. He cleared his throat…

"They raped me, all four of them. I heard noises in the background and when I was able to look, thinking someone was coming to help me, Coach was standing there, watching, and…well, he never touched me, but just himself…"

Wade sits on the floor under the window, rocking back and forth, hitting his head and crying… **"…THEN JUST GO**

···

AHEAD AND KILL ME…I DON'T CARE ANYMORE. I RATHER BE DEAD THAN TO KEEP REMEMBERING AND LISTENING TO YOU!"

Phyllis is in tears and terrified because she has never seen her son under attack before. Dr. Stewart sat next to her and held her hand until she went to sit with Wade under the window, in the hopes he would not stop talking.

"**I AM going to tell them who you are!** You are no longer the boss of me! I have been afraid of you most of my life. Even after I was grown, I was afraid of you. Even after you were dead, I was afraid of you. You let them rape me and the others, over and over. You did nothing. You just watched and enjoyed it. It's your fault I stop trusting adults. **You are worse than my grandfather. I never thought I would meet anyone worse than him and my mother's husband. But you beat them both.** You let them rape me until you were all dead."

Wade looked up at Dr. Stewart as if he forgot she and his mother were there.

"I remember the day they told us about the accident. There were no survivors. I went to the funerals. I watched people cry and talk about how great they were and how wonderful they were and how nice and kind the boys were and how their lives had been cut short…"

"LIES! LIES! LIES! I wanted to tell everyone the truth. I wanted to stand up in that church and tell them what you did and what they did. We all wanted to tell everyone the truth. But, we didn't. What difference would it have made? You can't punish the dead. As much as I hated talking to God, I did ask if He would punish ya'll. Make you walk around the earth in chains, like Jacob Marley. Obviously, He thought it more entertaining to punish me by putting you and your demon sons in my head all these years. Reminding me that if I ever tell, you would kill me. Well, now they know that you and your boys raped me and tormented me."

In the calmest voice she could muster, Dr. Stewart asked, "Wade, what are their names?"

Wade remained silent for a long moment. Still sitting under the window, still holding his head…

"Coach Alfred Philpot let them rape us, over and over and over, while he watched and…enjoyed it. Johnny, Mack, Hammerhead…his real name was George and Frank the Skank. They were horrible and no grown-ups believed us. They believed the coach. No grown-ups cared about what was happening to us."

Rocking back and forth, Wade cried, "So…kill me and get it over with…"

Just then, he lifted his head, looking directly in front of him, smiling, "Whisperers, you are still alive!? I thought he killed you."

...

"*Yes, we are alive, and it will all be over very soon.*"

"*Listen…*"

Then he heard his *Abuelita* say, **"Wade, nunca olvides que nunca te abandonará ni te olvidará de ti. Dile que lo necesitas ahora y vendrá, ahora."**

(*"Wade don't ever forget that He will never leave you or forget about you. Tell Him you need him now and He will come, now."*)

Wade, stood up, speaking in Spanish…

"*¡Abuelita, sigues aquí!*

Phyllis, still in shock, looked at Dr. Stewart, "Abuelita…that is what he called Marguerite's mother. She is one of the voices?

"*Yes, a comforting voice,*" *replied Dr. Stewart as she begins to translate for Phyllis,* "*Grandma, you are still here!*

"*Sí, pequeño.*" (*"Yes, little one."*)

"Abuelita, estás segura de que se preocupa por mí? ¿Estás seguro?"

Dr. Stewart continued to translate for Phyllis, "*Grandma, are you sure He cares about me? Are you sure?*"

"*Sí, estoy seguro…*" (*Yes, I am sure…*)

Again, Wade was no longer aware anyone else was in the room.

¡Jesús, te necesito ahora! ¡Por favor, haz que se vaya! ¡Por favor sácalo de mi cabeza!

Dr. Stewart continues, "*Jesus, I need you now! Please, make him go away! Please take him out of my head!*"

At that moment, Wade collapsed onto the floor, Phyllis ran and folded her son in her arms and started praying to God to save her son. Dr. Stewart called for the nurse.

When Wade regained consciousness, he was surrounded by folks in white coats. Then he saw his mother.

"Hey, you, you had us pretty worried there for a moment. How do you feel?"

"Like Thor hit me in the head with his hammer…" *The look on Phyllis' face told Wade she had no clue who Thor was.* "Mom, you have to get out more. The first chance I get, you will be watching the Thor movies with me…all three of them and any other Marvel movie you may have missed."

"That will be nice," smiled Phyllis.

"Doc, I'm still alive and I'm starving! Isn't that what the boy told Jesus when he raised him from the dead!" *Wade laughed a solid, hardy laugh. This was something he had not done in a very long time.*

His head did not hurt, and The Evil One was quiet.

Chapter 27
Everything Will Be Alright...

Never in a million years did Dr. Stewart expect the story to take the turn it did. Molested as a child. An adult who allowed it by watching and then threatening a terrified child not to tell. "Oh My Goodness..."

It was all Tiffany could do to maintain her composure while Wade told the horrible details of his ordeal. She wanted to scream, especially when he said the coach was dead. He should have gone to prison for the rest of his life so he could be continually raped by someone bigger and meaner than him. Now that he is dead, he should be burning in hell throughout eternity, if such a thing were possible.

Throughout the session, she paid attention to Wade's voice and posture, as well as what his mother was or was not doing, because she had to be ready at a moment's notice if either one of them fell apart, or if the voices actually attacked Wade. Ahead of the meeting, she asked the nurses and guards to be on standby, just in case. She was very happy the Christian guard was on duty today. Some of the guards did not make her job easy, which is what she needed today, cooperation from everyone involved.

Although she was poised and doing her job as a psychiatrist superbly, inside she was falling apart and prayed throughout the entire session that God would hold her together until Wade and Phyllis left her office and, hopefully, until she got home to her husband.

...

After Officer Jonathan and the nurse took Wade to the clinic and Phyllis had left for home, Tiffany locked her door, turn the overhead lights off, laid prostrate on the floor where she prayed and cried until there were no more tears left. She prayed:

> *"Oh God, is this why You put me in this profession? Did You think I would not help people heal through You if I had become a surgeon? Did You know that I would meet Mr. Wade and his voices and that today he would need my strength and his mother's*
> *strength! Did You know that today, he would realize just how much he needed You to overcome Satan's hold on him?"*
> *"Of course, You knew!"*
> *"Oh, I thank You…You are so AWESOME! You know the end from the beginning and, You knew I would not have been strong enough in the beginning to help him…AND…You knew I needed Mr. Wade so that I could heal."*
> *"You are so merciful…What would I do without You…"*

When she felt the strength come back into her, she stood up, picked up her keys and purse, and went home so she could lay in the arms of her husband until she was all better.

Tiffany's husband was not home when she arrived. There was a note on the chalkboard…"lym…brb," which is translated to mean "Love you more…Be right back". She hoped he was getting food, because she did not even have enough energy to make a peanut butter and jelly sandwich. She started her transformation ritual from prison psychiatrist to a normal woman waiting for the love of her life to come home. She sat in her chair on the porch with a glass of cranberry juice

...

and stared at nothing in particular. It was dusk and the night sounds were beginning. She was so happy she was able to convince her husband they did not have to live in the middle of the city. Their beautiful home sat on two acres of land with a beautiful landscape. She loved the space for her gardens, and he loved the space for his He-Shed and for his 'toys'.

She smiled, because in a couple years that spot over there by the willow trees will house a swing set and jungle gym. She is anxious to see the expression on his face when she tells him about the swing set, because, he does not know there will be a child playing on it along with his or her cousins and friends. When she thought about the life inside her, the anxiety she had about her past and Wade's past seem to fade away. She asked God to take care of Wade because he still had a long road ahead of him. She had more sessions with him in preparation for his new life outside of those walls.

When her husband pulled into the drive and exited his truck, she was so excited, not only to see him, but to see the Chinese food bags in his hand! As they ate dinner, without divulging what they talked about, she told him how her session with Wade was full of stress and anxiety, not only for him but for her also. He seemed to have had a stressful case with one of his patients also.

She decided this was the perfect time to tell him about her plans to put the swing set and jungle gym in the yard for their child. Even though he is a genius doctor, he can be a little slow sometimes. When he finally got it, he hugged her and kissed her with kisses full of tears and hugged her some more. And she hugged him and kissed him with kisses

...

full of tears and hugged him some more and told him how happy she was to be carrying his child. He went into the kitchen and returned with a steaming mug of Earl Grey tea with milk and honey — her favorite. She thanked God for giving her the perfect life, with the perfect husband.

Tiffany smiles when she remembered a verse in her vows… "Proverbs 18:22 (NIV) says, 'He who finds a wife finds what is good and receives favor from the Lord'. Well, I know that she who finds a good husband receives favor from the Lord."

Lord, I praise you and I thank you that I did not listen to my parents.

Chapter 28: *Session 29*
Silence…

Although Wade was no longer tormented by The Evil One and the other voices, he still had to manage bouts of bipolar and anxiety; and although he chose to reveal everything to Dr. Stewart and his mother, it was very embarrassing knowing someone else knows his darkest secret. He remained on his medication and on suicide alert under Dr. Stewart's care.

It has been two weeks since the last time he heard the voice of The Evil One. It has been two weeks since he had agonizing migraines. It has been two weeks since he told his darkest secret to another human. For the last two weeks, he has had peace of mind and peace in spirit. Even though he felt he was now living his best life, he was not totally out of the dark.

"Wade, how have you been since we last met? How does it feel to have a quiet mind? How does it feel living without your companions?"

"Doc, I am nearly sixty years old and I don't know if I remember a quiet mind since I was a child. Every now and again, I hear The Whisperers and Abuelita, but not the torment of the others. The other day I went to the church services for the first time since I have been here. Actually, the only time I've been in a church, since I was a child, was for funerals, and even then it was under orders from my mother or grandmother."

"How was it…the church service?"

"Well, I didn't fall over dead and the room didn't catch fire when I walked in, so I guess all was well. I actually enjoyed it. One of the men from the service asked if he could

...

sit with me in the dining room. It was weird having someone sit with me to eat."

"Why would that be weird?"

"Since I've been here, I usually sit alone to eat. I just prefer to be alone, not only in the courtyard, but everywhere. If The Voices started yelling, no one would know something was wrong with me. This time the only voice I heard was his. Actually, he reminded me of The Voices because he never shut up, except to put the fork in his mouth!" *Wade rolled his eyes...* "Jeez, OH MY GOODNESS! I thought I was gonna die! I hope he doesn't make it a habit of wanting to sit with me!" *Wade rolled his eyes again and shook his head...* "No, Thank You!"

"Wade, how are you feeling, emotionally, since the voices left? What about some of your other symptoms, especially the hallucinations? Have you had more episodes than before? Any new voices?"

Wade frowned as if he was annoyed at the questions...

"I don't know! I haven't heard any other voices. The Whisperers and Abuelita said they will be here if I ever need them. I guess they are waiting until I need them. The other day, during church services, I saw my grandmothers sitting in the pew across from me. They didn't say anything...just smiled. So, I guess, for now, I'm okay...I guess, I don't know."

"Excellent. Are you ready to discuss the events you told your mother and I?"

"**Why** do we need to discuss it!? I'm sure my mother wants to *'discuss'* it too. I really don't see the point. It was when I was a kid. I did what you said I needed to do. I conquered my fears. The Evil One is dead. I'm still alive, and I am now the boss of me. Isn't that what you wanted me to learn. I have no reason to rehash any of it…***ever again!***"

"Yes, it is what I wanted you to learn. I am very proud of you and what you have accomplished over the last two years and especially over the last few weeks. However, you do know those boys were his victims also, right? They were probably just as afraid of him as you and the others were."

"Okay…maybe so. What has it to do with me?"

"Those boys were the loud voices, weren't they?"

"Yes."

"Why did you allow them to torment you all of these years? I have to wonder if it was for more than fear. I was really surprised The Evil One was not your grandfather or your stepfather, and I expect your mother wonders the same thing. Have you ever heard their voices after they died?"

"No."

"Really…"

"You don't hear many stories about Satan personally attacking people. There is always someone else, doing his

…

dirty work. When all of that was happening to me, I tried to tell my grandfather. He said I deserved it and anything else that happened to me. When I said I would talk to my parents and grandmother, he said nobody cared about me. He said he was sure I did something to warrant the abuse. So as Coach allowed the boys to do what they did, I just said nothing."

"Are you saying your grandfather knew you were being molested and bullied and he did nothing; he told no one?"

"Yes."

"I told you he was an evil man. I guess I never heard his voice because he was satisfied with the torment caused by The Evil One and his Boys. Besides, I'm sure he is too busy trying to figure out why heaven is so hot!" *Wade had to laugh.* "I remember once he told me he would make sure I never made it to heaven, like he had some sort of inside deal with God as to who would or would not get into heaven. I told him if he sent me to hell, he would be there to greet me. He was furious. I laughed and walked out of the room."

"You have always had control over the other symptoms related to schizophrenia, except the voices. Now that you have overcome, what will you do if they return or if others try to enter…such as your grandfather or stepfather?

Wade sat there, rubbing his head, as was his habit when he was thinking…

"If they return? What do you mean, return? Doc, do you know this song. He started to sing…

'Never would have made it, never could have made it without You…

I'm stronger. I'm wiser. I'm better, so much better.

When I look back over all You brought me through,

I can see that You were the One I held on to…'."

"Anyways, when bad thoughts or voices attack me, all I have to do is what my dad and Abuelita told me to do…remember where my help comes from and who can fight for me. I was taught all of this as a child, but I let my issues make me forget it. I won't forget again. *He rubbed his head and face…* I'm just saying, I denied myself the opportunity to have a relationship with Him, *as he pointed to the ceiling,* and with my family. I chose to allow myself to become cold, uncaring and ruthless. Never again."

"Now that you have conquered this hill in your struggle, what will you replace it with?"

"What do you mean…replace it with?"

"There's a passage in the Gospels, Matthew and Luke, about when a person is freed from an impure spirit. If they just clean themselves up, but don't replace the negative spirit with something spiritually positive, the spirit will return with seven of its deadliest friends. Have you ever heard the story before?"

"No."

"It is found in Matthew 12:43-45 and Luke 11:24-26. Here, I'll write it down for you."

"Once you realized you were not alone, you believed your prayers would work. Now you are rid of The Evil One, his Boys and any other evil voices which may have been tormenting you. However, if you do not fill the void in your mind with good thoughts and good activities, they will return, along with your grandfather, your stepfather and who knows who else."

Dr. Stewart paused to let it all soak in...

"Remember this, just because the water is calm doesn't mean there are no crocodiles."

"It was a good thing you went to the services the other day. However, you have to fill your mind continuously with positive things, learning positive ways to cope with stress and anxiety, find positive hobbies, studying the Bible and renewing broken relationships. You have already started with your mother and Antonio, however, I'm sure there are many more, especially, Akina."

"When you go home, you must avoid old negative energy people and old stomping grounds, as well as anything that has the potential to set you back—no street drugs or alcohol. Although you have been clean while in here, it's really easy to return to using. This is why you will be required to attend narcotic and alcohol anonymous meetings at a drug and alcohol rehabilitation center. It will help you reenter society with a clean body and a clean spirit."

Wade started to feel a little panicky, "Doc, once I leave here, I won't be seeing you anymore, will I? I will certainly **refuse** to see another therapist." *He put both feet flat on the floor and crossed his arms, mimicking a tantrum...*

"Oh no, Wade, that's not what I'm saying, although you are a lot stronger than you realize. However, I'm just preparing you for the transition from here to your new life outside."

"Oh," *Wade breathes a sigh,* "it's a lot to remember to do and don't do. I've been talking to my brother about coming home. When I told him I would probably just go to a halfway house for a little while, he said no. He said I would be moving into my old apartment. My dad built a house for homeless veterans who worked for him. It would be their permanent home for as long as they needed. Even though I was never military or homeless, he set aside an apartment on the top floor for me. I stayed there when I was sick. Otherwise, I always had my own place; but my dad kept it for me. I was really shocked when Antonio told me my room was still there." *Again, Wade wiped his face...*

"I remember you saying regardless of how horrible you treated Antonio, he was always kind to you."

Wade sat there, biting his fingernail, which he had never done before. This was new. He just stared into nothing...

"Huh, yeah, that's something isn't it? At my worst, he was always at his best. I'm sure his mother and Abuelita use

...

215

to talk to him a lot. Maybe they told him no matter what, he had to be Joseph because I was a combination of all eleven of the other brothers."

Wade smiled, sat back in his chair and crossed his legs. Another first.

"Okay, Doc, so what's next!"

"Thou wilt keep him in perfect peace, whose mind is stayed on thee:

because he trusteth in thee." (KJV)

Isaiah 28:3

Chapter 29
A Decision To Be Made…

The week before Wade was to be released, Maria called a meeting with Antonio, Lizanne, Esabelle and their lawyer, Mr. Johnson.

As the Chief Financial Officer of the company, Maria had a concern about what Wade's role would be in MMTrucking. Although he had paid his debt to society and had gone through extensive psychiatric care, she still had a concern about his ability to function in the company. Like Lizanne, Maria had not been to see Wade once while he was in prison. She decided his bitterness was not something she chose to subject herself to. Also, it had been her and Lizanne's responsibility to clean up the financial and operational chaos Wade had left in his wake. If it had not been for Justin and the rest of the financial staff, it would have been much, much harder for Maria.

Maria, Lizanne and their staff were putting out fires every day. It seemed that, as one fire was extinguished, another one blazed. It took one of the two years Wade was in prison to start moving forward again.

The conversation among the siblings concerning should they or should they not allow Wade back into the business went from calm to frantic when Mr. Johnson reminded them of the old problems they had to endure because of Wade and presented them with new possible legal ramifications of making him an active partner. It was the good, the bad and the ugly of the love-hate story of Wade and MMTrucking.

...

At the end of the meeting, they came to an agreement they all could live with, including Wade.

Chapter 30: *Session 33*
Going Home…

Wade met with Dr. Stewart for the last time, as an inmate. He was actually relieved when she told him he could continue to see her as a private client if he chose to do so.

On their last visit, she recapped where he started and the progress he has made. As they discussed some of the hurdles yet ahead, she reminded him he is stronger than his fears. She reminded him he must work to fill his mind with positive thoughts and activities so bad voices won't have a home to re-occupy.

"Doc, I've heard a lot of stories about folks getting out of jail and not being able to get anything done in the world. No one wants to give them an opportunity to get back on their feet. I've known people in that situation. A couple of them ended up driving for me when I was in the trucking business. That didn't work out too good."

"Wade, everyone gets a second chance. It's what they do with the opportunity that matters."

"I guess you are right Doc. See you on the outside."

If he had been allowed to hug her he would have, but it wasn't allowed, so he just walked out of her office…for the last time.

With the officer by his side, Wade walked down the hall with this one or that one saying so long. He walked through one door…SLAM! He walked through another door…SLAM! CLICK!

…

Although he was walking at what he thought was a normal pace, he felt as if he was moving in slow motion. He wondered how men who have lived inside these gates for much longer than him felt at this moment. He walked out of the first gate…CLANG…then the second gate…CLANG!

Finally, as he was about to walk through the last gate, the guard gave him a gift, a brand new Men's Study Bible (NIV). The note written inside said, "…I come that they might have life, and that they might have it more abundantly." John 10:10b. Wade recognized the text because his dad quoted it both times he tried to commit suicide…when Satan tried to kill him. He read the inscription again as he thanked the guard for the bible and for saving his life. They did the man hug…shoulder bump and three solid pats on the back.

Once Wade had cleared the last gate and was standing on the walkway, the guard raised his hand toward the tower and it began to slide closed, sounding as if it were dragging very slowly, screeching and scraping across the track. Then the last CLANG! … CLICK! Then…silence.

Wade stood still as he heard the last click of the gates closing and locking him out. A moment ago, two and a half years of moments ago, those same clanking gates locked him in, securing the world from the threat of him. Now, the last click thrust him back into that same world. "So," he wondered, "does this mean he is now among the protected?"

Wade thinking to himself, but unknowingly using his outside voice, "It is amazing how the oxygen feels so different in my

...

lungs while breathing on the outside of the gate. I'm sure it's the same air, but it sure feels different, it smells different, it even tastes different!"

"Breathe in…Breathe out, breathe in…breathe out…slowly…don't hyperventilate trying to fill your lungs up too quickly with this new air. Wade almost panicked, looking around him knowing there was no one, "Huh…whose there…whose voice is this giving me instructions!?" *He smiled big when he realized the voice in his head was one he is still trying to get accustomed to…his own.* "Nice!"

His anxiety level was pretty high. He wanted to feel free, but all he could feel at this moment was fear. He wondered if Doc could see him standing on the walkway, afraid to put one foot in front of the other. He wondered if she realized, that, at that moment, he was feeling completely alone, and kind of naked. Two years ago, he and his voices walked in and today, he walked out, alone. No voices, just him. He now knows what it felt like to have a huge burden lifted. Yesterday he remembered the words of a song he used to play in church, when he was playing his saxophone…when he was going to church, "…burdens are lifted at Calvary, Jesus is very near." *He laughed out loud because, everything he had forgotten about Jesus and church, he started remembering after the Evil One and The Boys died. He will have to get himself a new saxophone.*

He had no idea how long he stood outside of the gate, in the same spot, on the walkway, before he noticed the two cars parked at the curb. Patiently standing by the cars were six people, watching him. At the same moment, he realized who they were, one of them shouted, "Why are we standing here looking all 'Color Purple!!!'" "Wade! Wade!" she was yelling as she ran towards him with her arms open wide.

When he heard her voice, he immediately had flashbacks of her running towards him when she was young. He always knew his baby sister had unconditional love for him.

He dropped his bag and scooped Esabelle up and swung her around like he did when they were kids. Well, not exactly like when they were kids because now he is a lot older and spinning around was not always a good idea.

Then, he was surrounded by his other two siblings, Antonio and Maria. They hugged him individually and then the four of them group hugged for a minute. The spouses stayed at the car to give them this moment. Someone snapped a few pictures. Eventually, they were all in the cars headed to his favorite restaurant for lunch…IHOP!

As they sat waiting for their food to arrive, Wade looked at his siblings and their spouses. Everyone laughing and talking over each other about the family events that occurred during the last two years. Marriages, babies, college, etc. He sipped on his sweet tea to keep from crying. Then he heard his name…

"Wade, Wade! man, where is your head!"

"I'm sorry, I was listening to you all telling two years' worth of family news. Some of it I've heard and some I didn't. I was thinking about how much family time I missed while living in my madness."

No one said anything. They just gave him their undivided attention. He looked away for a moment, looking at nothing in particular. Then he cleared his throat, drank more tea and continued.

"I've done some horrible things…" *Esabelle was interrupting him, but he stopped her.* "Let me finish. I have always loved the three of you, although nothing I did could have proven it. I wasn't there when Antonio and Maria were born. However, I had the privilege of being there when Esabelle came home. I often think about California and I wish I could have had that life always, but it wasn't in the cards for me. I could easily blame it on the illness, which would be partially true. I could have made better, more positive decisions. *He used the napkin to wipe his face and head…*

"Antonio, you had something I never had privilege to…a hands-on relationship with our dad. The three years in California were the best, consecutive, three years of my life where I was with family who loved me unconditionally and I loved them unconditionally. It was not your fault I did not have a fulltime life with dad. The people whose fault it was…I couldn't do anything to them for the pain they caused, so I took it out on you. Yes, it was my fault dad gave you MMTrucking, but I allowed my jealousy and anger to control my decision making. The things I did, especially

···

trying to ruin the business, was despicable, and I have asked your forgiveness before, but I want to ask you again, in the presence of our family, because everything I did not only affected you and me, but the entire family, including spouses, especially, Lizanne."

At this point, everyone is tearing up and wiping their faces. Maria and Esabelle's husbands held them as close as the chairs would allow, with one arm, and wiping their faces with the other. Lizanne placed her hand on top of Antonio's and did not move it until he put his arm around her.

Still sitting in the IHOP, with nosey folk trying to figure out what was going on, Wade continued...

"I know this might not be the best place for such a conversation, but..." *He was interrupted this time by Maria, "You think!" They all laughed.*

"I would like, with you all's permission, to finish because when we get home, I want to be able to start my new life with a clean slate." *They all nodded in agreement.*

"Lizanne, I ask for your personal forgiveness because I pretty much interfered with your family on many levels. I urged Jason to mistrust God after your mom passed. And then I did try to pull him in on my scheme when he joined MMTrucking. Both times I was selfish, interjecting my misery and my dislike and distrust of God on him. When I see him, I will apologize to him, if he will allow it."

...

He paused, just long enough to see Lizanne nod her head in agreement. At that moment, Lizanne knew God had answered her prayers. "Yes, thank you and please forgive me for being so mean to you."

"You had every right," Wade nodded, "But thank you much."

"Antonio knows about this; however, I want to tell you all. I had an "encounter" in prison—sort of my own Damascus Road experience. Jesus, Dad and Abuelita helped me defend myself and stand up to the demon voices living in my head for most of my teen and all of my adult life. Dad reminded me of a conversation he and I had when he reminded me Satan was trying to kill me in my sins. Abuelita told me to pray and ask Jesus to help me."

Again, Maria interrupted, "Are you saying Dad and Abuela spoke to you? Why don't they speak to us?" as she pointed towards Antonio and Esabelle.

"Wade replied, "I don't know. Maybe they felt you all were safe and would be fine. You all were not dealing with the issues I was." *Wade hung his head and wiped his face again.*

"The whole ordeal is a very long story I may tell another day. What's important is when I asked God to help me and take them away, most of The Voices left at the same time. I couldn't hear them at all, until the worst one returned. My therapist and my mom helped me abolish him. He had

...

tormented me when he was alive and continued to torment me after his death."

He could tell by their looks he would eventually have to tell them what happened to him…but not today.

"I no longer have to live with the bad voices in my head. My spirit is clean now. My mind is on creating a new, good life for myself. I'm praying again, reading and studying the bible. I know everyone thinks most inmates, *as he put up two fingers for the "quote" sign,* "find Jesus" long enough to get out of prison, but I'm trying to renew my relationship with Him and I would like to continue with the relationship, as well as start a new relationship with you all and the rest of the family…if you all will have me."

And, as if this was a signal to chime in, they all started talking at once about everything.

Again, Wade watched his siblings with new eyes. He knew he had a long road ahead of him, but he thanked God for this second chance. Doc had given him a poem entitled 'Our Deepest Fear.' As we are liberated from our own fear, our presence automatically liberates others. Wade prayed his presence will be a blessing for him and others, not a burden…not a nightmare.

Chapter 31
The Letter…

Wade walked around the well-manicured yard of his mom's house looking at the shrubs, trees, flowers and the little winter garden she had in the back. Peppers, collards, sweet potatoes, kale, swiss chard, arugula and mustard. She even had some herbs still growing from the summer. He thought out loud, "I wonder who's keeping up her yard. Hmmmm… Fe-Fi-Fo-Fum!…"

As he walked from the yard into the kitchen, he sat at the table watching his mom. He thought about all the time he wasted being angry at her. Now, he wonders how much time he has left. She is very active and still gets around on her own. However, as she would say, 'her insides is still 76 and there are days when she moves slower than normal'."

"Wade, it is so good to see you sitting at this table." Phyllis interrupted his thoughts as she Mama Bear hugged him.

"Yes, it is," *Wade chimed in.*

On the table, next to the hot yeast rolls, butter and molasses, was a box. Deep inside, Wade had a feeling he did not want to know what was in it, knowing he had no choice but to know what was in it.

Phyllis touched the box and looked at him, "In this box are bits and pieces of the life of your daughter." As she walked out the back door with a pan of rolls in her hand, she smiled and said, "It is time you became acquainted, so, I will leave you to her and your rolls. I'm going to visit Mr. Evans." Wade looked at the pan of rolls in her hand and frowned...

"And who is Mr. Evans?"

As Phyllis stepped into her yard, she laughed and then yelled over her shoulder, "My neighbor."

Sliding his chair back from the table, Wade yelled out the door, "Maybe I should go with you and meet this Mr. Evans."

"No darlin'. You handle your business with that box. I'll be back shortly. You'll meet Mr. Evans soon enough." Laughing and shaking her head as she crossed the yard, "chil'ren!"

Avoiding the box, Wade helped himself to a roll floating in butter and molasses. This was a common meal for him growing up. Today it was a delicacy, because he had not eaten any since long before he went to prison. He closed his eyes as he savored the flavors of the warm bread, the melted butter and the sweetest molasses he's had in a very long time. He didn't know how long he sat there with his eyes closed, but when he opened them, the first thing he saw was...the box.

As he pulled the box towards him, he wanted to throw it into the trash, however he knew this was another fear he had to face. So many things he messed up and missed out on because of his fear, and his anger, and his jealousy. There were times when more than one or all of these emotions caused destruction on his mind, body and spirit...as well as the well-being of others.

He thumbed through the pictures of Rebeca, her husband, Michelle and, of course, Akina. His head began to hurt as he read parts

...

of the journals Rebeca left. Notes about their love and how he sent her away. Notes about his nightmares and The Evil One. Notes about how she prayed for the strength to help him defeat him, notes about how he turned his back on her because the Evil One told him to.

"She knew? ... **She knew? ... Oh God! She knew!?**"

Wade sat back in the chair with his hands over his eyes as if doing so would somehow erase what he had read. He remembered her telling him about his nightmare, which he shrugged off and pretended it was nothing.

"After growing up in hell, where live men ruined every aspect of my childhood, how stupid was I to let dead men ruin my alive life! Oh God!...if I had listened to You...or my mother...or my father. If I had listened to Rebeca! If I had let anyone help me, where would I have ended up? I'm sure not just finding out I have a 19-year-old daughter!"

Wade stood up and walked across the kitchen and stood by the window, like he used to do in Dr. Stewart's office when he was stressed.

He took a deep breath and sighed, "This is all too much."

Wade drank a Root Beer, another favorite he did not have for the last two and a half years. He walked down the hallway, looking at how nicely his mom had decorated her little house.

When her mother needed care, Phyllis sold her house and moved back to Beaufort to take care of her. He thought about how this house was a house of misery when he was a child and how he was treated like a

...

mistake...a goblin child born on Halloween. Today, except for a few pictures and artifacts, no one would know this was the same house.

Phyllis loved Christmas and, even though it was a couple weeks before Thanksgiving, there were already hints of Christmas here and there. Wade laughed, "This house is so much happier now that Mom has breathed life into it."

He looked at the pictures on the wall, of family members, even Grandfather. There were pictures from every generation of their family.

As he walked towards the end of the hall leading into the front room, he stopped and almost choked on his drink. There, on the wall were three framed photographs. The first was a picture of him and his mother taken when he graduated from high school. The next was a picture of his mom and Rebeca. He smiled when he remembered when it was taken.

The third picture took his breath away. It was a picture of his mother and her beautiful granddaughter. She was his mother's twin, her mini-her. This picture made Akina real for him, seeing her and his mother taking a selfie made him weak in his knees. He stood there for a moment, ordering tears to stay in their ducts. He was about to wipe his face when he realized he had been walking with a letter in his hand. It was addressed to him. He sat down and opened it...

> "Dear Daddy, I know you might be afraid to meet me because you didn't know about me and because of who knows how many other reasons. I don't know why Rebeca thought it was a good idea to keep you from me, maybe she was trying to protect me from something. It is sad no one will ever know.

...

230

I have to tell you I am also very scared about all of this, because I don't know if you will accept me. Nevertheless, let me just say this. I don't know who you were, but I can tell you who I am and what I do know. I know you are my dad and I want to have a relationship with you, even if you decide you don't want to have a relationship with me.

Let me tell you a little bit about me, so that if you choose not to accept me, you will know what you will be missing out on.

And for several pages, Akina outlined her life for Wade. Every tooth that fell out, every friend, every important event in school. She told him how she has been on the A/B honor roll all of her life. She told him what she was studying, as a sophomore in college.

She told him about her cousin Michelle and how they have more frequent flyer miles than most adults, because their adventurous parents made sure they were world traveled.

She told him about her boyfriend (singular). She thought it important to make sure he knew she only had one boyfriend. She told him she and her boyfriend were still virgins, by choice, and planned to remain so until marriage to each other or whomever.

She told him how much she loved God and church. Her mother was not much into church, but her auntie and uncle took her every week to church with them. Sometimes she went on Saturday and Sunday.

She told him how sad she was when her mom and stepdad died and how angry she was at her mother when she found out she could have had her father to hold her through it all.

She told him about meeting her Grandma Phyllis and how much she loves her.

At the end of the letter she wrote, "I can't be angry with you for not knowing about me.

The thing I can hope for now is that you will allow us to start from now.

...

Much Love always, your Baby Girl, Phyllis Akina Williams."

Chapter 32
Family Reunion…

Wade and Phyllis were fortunate to find a parking spot not too far from the entrance of the campus library. Wade stood holding the car door, mainly because he had this sudden urge to get back in and drive back to Beaufort. However, he knew, this would be the most important day of his life. Today, his daughter is one of the keynote speakers for a collegiate Science, Technology, Engineering and Math (STEM) conference being held on her college campus. Today, would be the first time he would see her, in person. So, he could not leave.

Phyllis wanted to sit on the front row, just like she does at church. Wade was happy she agreed to sit a few rows back. He hoped she would not spot them until after her speech. He kept saying he didn't want to make her nervous, but it was really him who was full of anxiety.

Although neither he nor Phyllis had a clue as to what any of the speakers were talking about, they paid close attention to Akina's speech and tried to follow her speech coupled with this graph and the other graph. In the end, all of the students seemed to know actually what they were talking about, as well as most of the audience.

When it was over, Wade asked his mother could they just sit for a moment, so he could get his insides in order. For a moment, he was worried the anxiety would make him sick to his stomach.

Just as he was deciding he would live, he heard, "Grandma! Grandma! Did you like my speech? I was so nervous! I'm sure you were bored out of your mind with all of the…"

Then she saw him. So tall she had to really tilt her head back to see the top of him. And then he saw her. Looking as if someone took her mother's DNA and her grandmother's DNA and spliced them together to make this beautiful young woman.

Phyllis decided the proper thing to do was to take the lead and introduce them. Otherwise, she feared they would be standing there for quite some time.

"Akina, this is my son, Timothy Wade Martin, your father. Everyone calls him Wade. Wade, this is my granddaughter, Phyllis Akina Williams, your daughter. Everyone calls her Akina." And then she stepped to the side to allow them room to do whatever they were going to do.

The tears were flowing down Akina's face as she looked from her grandmother to her father. Then she practically leaped into his arms and held on to him as if she were lost and he found her.

Wade had not felt this kind of love, ever. As the tears flowed, he pulled her away from him so he could look at her. He pulled a handkerchief from his pocket and wiped her face. He put his arms around her and hugged her some more.

Phyllis, Mr. Evans and Akina's boyfriend continued to stand to the side and give them their space. Phyllis thanked God she lived long enough to see her son become a parent.

...

Wade never thought he would ever be a parent and now, enveloped in his arms is his daughter, and although he just met her, he loved her with the everlasting love he figured could only be felt by a parent, because, his heart has never felt like this, not even for Rebeca.

Finally, more introductions were made as Akina introduced her boyfriend to her father.

Phyllis suggested they leave the auditorium so the people could lock up and go home to their own families. There was a little diner around the corner where they could get to know each other better and get something to eat.

While everyone chattered around the table, Wade just looked at his family, even the boyfriend and Mr. Evans, and thanked God for this day. He was the prodigal son returned and despite his horrible life, he is being blessed every day. As he looked at Akina, he began to understand God's love for him. As they walked towards the car, the only thing he could say was, "Thank You God, for having mercy on me," as he wrapped his arms around his baby girl.

Chapter 33
Giving Thanks…

*"…we had to celebrate and be glad, because this brother of
yours was dead and is alive again; he was lost and is found." Luke
15:32 (NIV)*

Thanksgiving for the Martin Family was a major production
started at least two months earlier. This year the Millennials are the
"coordinators" of the menu and the deciders of who would bring what.
Praise God they were raised on real food. They were responsible for
contacting family members concerning what they were bringing to the
feast. Macaroni and Cheese (3 pans); Green Bean Casserole (2 pans);
Sweet Potato Custard (4 pans); Potato Salad (2 bowls), Rice and Peas
(2 pans); A kettle of Gumbo; Greens (3 pans); Turkeys (1 fried / 1
baked); Drunk Chicken (3); Crab Pots (3); Sweet Potato Pies (5);
Pound Cake (2), punch and whatever else someone brings for dessert.
And somebody always brought something that wasn't on the menu. They
were instructed NEVER to let Sally bring anything that needed to be
cooked cause everybody, but her knows she cain't cook. Those greens she
brought last year came out of the ground and on to the plate…not a drop
of water or salt pass through them – **horrible and dirty**! Tell her to
bring 12 packs of **STORE BOUGHT** dinner rolls.

Now the day has come and family members from near and far
are dropping off pots and pans full of food, already hot and ready to eat.
Thanksgiving was always, always, always at Grammee's house, Marcus'

...

mother, and Matriarch of the Martin Family. As the family grew, Marcus remodeled his childhood house, where his mother still lived. He added a couple more bedrooms, a closed in deck and a state of the art kitchen. Grammee hosted many soirees in her day. However, the biggest and most remembered was Thanksgiving. This year Grammee is ninety-six years old. She has outlived her husband and both of her sons, as well as two grandchildren. Theodore Roosevelt was the President when she was born. She survived the Great Depression, Jim Crow, the Civil Rights Movement and the election and re-election of the first Black president of the United States – President Barak Obama.

She was a wonderful storyteller. The children all enjoyed listening to her talk about "way back when she and her friends sat, every day, at the counter of Woolworth until they served them." Once one of the children asked her if she had ever been beaten and arrested at Woolworth. She smiled and told them those were perilous times. Now, she is quiet most of the time. She says she has pretty much said everything she had to say. Now she says she wants to save her voice for when she talks to Jesus, face to face.

The family did not want to put her in a nursing home so Antonio and Lizanne gave their house to Jason and Grace and they now live with Grammee and care for her.

Thanksgiving Dinner was really Thanksgiving Brunch because everyone arrived about 1:30 or 2:00 to eat and then go outside for the famous Martin Family Flag Foosball Game and a few other games designed to run down lunch so they would be ready to come back for seconds and TV football, Spades and Dominos.

So, food was brought in and the designated "receivers" were receiving, warming up and placing dishes in their proper places on the tables. Everyone was laughing and having a wonderful time getting caught up from the last time.

The door opened and there was an immediate hush in the entire house. The kitchen crew realized the silence and came out to see what was going on. And then, just as quickly as there was silence, there was a roar of "Hey man…what's up!" and "Uncle Wade…Uncle Wade" and "Yo man…you don't look like you missed too many meals while you was up in there!" and of course, "Look man, I would'a come see 'bout cha but…followed by whatever came after 'but…'"

For the first five or ten minutes, Wade was completely overwhelmed. He was almost mechanical, shaking this hand, hugging that neck, patting the heads of little ones that, although they had no clue who he was, felt they were required to hug his legs.

Life returned to him when, as he turned into the front room, he saw his grandmother. Tears welled up in his eyes as he went over to her. Thank God there was a chair next to her because he was sure if he got down on his knees he'd never get back up.

Because her eyesight wasn't what it used to be, when he touched her hands she put her hands on his face.

"Grammee it's me, Wade. I'm so sorry I…"

...

"Shhh boy, everything is alright now. I prayed and God told me I would see you before I died." As those nearby stood silently and watched, she waved her hand over them and said, "All of my other babies have been here with me, all but you. I just kept praying and kept looking and kept asking about you. You are home now. Everything is alright."

Wade hung his head in silence for a moment. Then, while tears were flowing, he told his grandmother how sorry he was for the heartache he caused her and the family. He told her that her prayers saved his life and he would never leave her again.

In all of the excitement, no one noticed Wade's mother slip in and walking in behind her was Akina. When Wade looked up and saw her, he motioned for her to come over to him.

"Grammee, I want you to meet the only good thing that came out of my life. This is your great-granddaughter. Her name is Akina."

Akina moved to the other side of her great-grandmother, bent down and hugged her. Grammee's arms felt like medicine to Akina.

"Stand-up straight child so I can get a good look at you. Oh my goodness, just look at you." She looked at Wade and asked, "Who is her mama, is it..."

"Yes ma'am, her mama is Rebeca."

"I met your mama a couple times when we came to visit Wade." She motioned to several of the ones standing by, "Go and tell

...

everyone to come in here. From the kitchen and outside too. Tell them all to come now."

When everyone came into the house, she said, "Today is a special day in the history of The Martin family. Today, God has blessed me with a new great-granddaughter and a new great-great-grandson." She motioned for them to bring her the new baby.

"This family has been blessed beyond measure. We have lost family members, but God has been steadily opening windows and giving us a new family to carry on our legacy. I'm not gonna be here much longer and when I talk to Jesus, I will ask him to continue to pour down blessings on each and every one of you."

"You are all my babies and I love every last one of you. Even those young'uns over there with their eyes rolling because they would rather be in a corner with their eyes glued to their phones on Snapchat … Yes…I know what Snapchat is", as she smiled at one of her granddaughters who took the time to teach her how to use her cellphone! "We all are here for a reason and it is up to us to decide what we will do with the time God gives us between the day we are born and the day we die…that dash. Use that time wisely for once it's up, you will never have another chance to fix anything."

"Anyway, I love all of you and this young lady right here will need all the love any one person can get from a family."

"Wade, take your baby and introduce her to her family. You and I can talk later."

...

Akina hugged her again. Then Wade commenced with the introductions. Naturally, everyone was in shock because no one knew Wade had a daughter; however, they all received, or pretended to receive Akina into the family.

Before any plate was fixed, it was tradition for everyone to say a quick statement about what they are thankful for since the last year. Grammee was good at cutting people off if they got long-winded. "Jonesee, please, I'm 96 years old and I'd like to eat before I die, thank you very much!'

When it was Wade's turn to say what he was thankful for, all he said was, "I was lost and now I'm found."

During dinner, *Wade watched his family as they interacted with each other. He thought about what his grandmother said about the dash. In his wallet was the poem Dr. Stewart gave him. He reads it often, especially when he is full of anxiety. It gives him strength for one more day.*

And today, he has read it four times reminding himself that, even with the anxiety, it is a very good day to be with his family…and allow them to be with him.

Chapter 34
A New Life…

When all of the Thanksgiving festivities were over, and everyone going home went home, he sat in what quickly became his favorite chair in his room. On the wall was a picture of Marcus, with Wade next to him and Antonio sitting on Wade's shoulders. Wade smiled when he remembered that day.

Throughout his time with Dr. Stewart, she encouraged him to keep a journal of all of his old memories and episodes with the voices. She told him if he kept them in his head they would continue to take on a life of their own and control his actions. However, writing takes his thoughts, including fears, out of his head and puts them onto paper where he can see them, evaluate their importance, and then decide how to reprimand or reward… himself.

Even though he is free, he decided it good to continue his journals. Only now his journals will be of the new memories he is making, including how he is handling his fears and anxieties. He was happy to write that today was a very good day.

He spent as much time as possible with Akina, trying not to smother her. He would attend her events, no matter how big or small, because he wanted to somehow, make up for lost time.

He met Akina's Uncle Barnell and Auntie Opal, and as Akina had warned him, went to church with both of them…Uncle on Sabbath and Auntie on Sunday. Opal grilled him with a fierceness until Barnell just had to ask her to leave the man alone. Opal made it clear Rebeca carried a pain for him all her life and she did not intend to let that happen with Akina.

"Auntie…", Akina exclaimed. Wade chimed in quickly, "No, Baby-girl, it's okay. Your auntie has every right to be skeptical of me. I broke your mother's heart and because of it, I missed out on all of your life to this point. However, I will not be missing out on another day from now on."

Eventually, Opal felt comfortable enough accept him in Akina's life and tell him all about Rebeca, her crazy and trifling family and Akina.

A couple weeks before Christmas, he had an appointment to see Dr. Stewart. He told her there were no new voices. He told her all about his Akina and the rest of the family. He was able to show her pictures of his daughter and talk about her accomplishments. This was a new high he had not experienced before, and he was already addicted.

He…was a proud Dad.

...

He told her, quite unexpectedly, his siblings asked him if he wanted to join the business. He had not considered getting involved with the business and he was amazed they would even consider it after all he had done. After a week of thinking and praying, he decided against having an active role in MMTrucking. He knew he had more healing to do and something that tedious would only cause anxiety for him. So, he turned down the opportunity for an active role and accepted the role of a silent partner.

As the weeks turned into months, Wade began to feel more and more comfortable in his new life without The Voices. There were times when he would talk to Abuelita or his dad or The Whisperers... even though they did not respond, which was okay with him because it meant he was managing on his own.

He started going to church with Antonio, Lizanne and Jamie. He was surprised to learn the people who kept aggravating him in prison and who left the Message Magazine in his room were members of their church.

He mentioned to Lizanne he needed help understanding some of the things he read, and she introduced him to Janice Colberts, who became his bible study partner.

Ironically, Janice was employed by MMTrucking, so she knew who Wade was and was aware of some of his issues. Something about her made him comfortable enough

...

to tell her what she didn't know. They met every week for six months. During those six months, he learned how to love himself and love Jesus.

During the next six months, he also learned what it felt like to love another woman. He had not loved any woman since Rebeca. And so, he and Janice courted.

He smiled when he remembered asking God if he was ready for a wife, and God came through for him. He and Janice were united during a small family wedding. He never knew this kind of happiness until he saw her walk down the aisle towards him. He remembered how happy Marcus was when Marguerite walked towards him all those years ago. Now, he understood what his father tried to teach him all of his life. *"Love conquers all."* He was 61 years old.

Chapter 35
Wade Renewed...

Wade regretted the years he wasted fueled by jealousy, hatred and fear, however, he learned a valuable lesson he was able to teach his grandchildren. He taught them what he called Wade's Rules for Happiness:

(1)   Always remember what they have been taught about Jesus' love for them, and that prayer always changes things.

(2)   Jesus will never leave them nor forsake them, no matter what they have done or may do.

(3)   Family is bigger than blood. Family is your name, your reputation and your legacy. Everything done...or not done...reflects back on the family...good, bad or indifferent.

(4)   No matter how difficult a task might seem, they have the strength within them to overcome any obstacle.

(5)   And most importantly, always, always, always remember they can always tell their Pop-Pop anything and as long as there is oxygen in my lungs, I will love them with a forever love.

...

With the help of Dr. Stewart, Wade eventually used his journals and his sessions with her to write his memoirs about his life and his Rules of Happiness. His book helped many people understand that everyday people have issues in their life which, if not faced and handled, will overtake them.

His book became a best seller and launched him on a new adventure, as an author.

Wade lived half of his life believing he was a mistake and his punishment was to suffer with schizophrenia, die in his sins and lose the most precious thing to him, his salvation. When he allowed himself to remember the Jesus of his childhood, he became a new person with a new life.

Wade lived to be 93 years old. He and Janice were married for thirty-one years before he died. Attending his funeral were family and friends who loved him, as well as people whose lives had been changed because of his story. The last line of his obituary read…

"Train up a child in the way he should go; and when he is old, he will not depart from it."
Proverbs 22:6 (KJV)

The Dash was written by Laura Ellis in 1996. The poem can be found at https://thedashpoem.com/

Our Deepest Fear, from the book "A Return to Love: Reflections on the Principles of A Course in Miracles" was written by Marianne Williamson in 1996 and can be found at http://storage.cloversites.com/fellowshipchurch2/documents/poem%20-%20Our%20Deepest%20Fear.pdf

They can also be found on Dr. AudreyAnn's website https://www.transitionlifecoach4u.com/inspiration--empowerment-and-affirmations.html

...

Epilogue
Some Facts About Schizophrenia

There are many people in America living with Schizophrenia. Although people know schizophrenia exist, there is little known about what it is, the effect it has on the individual and society, as well as, what are some of the commonly used treatments?

Because society is not well educated concerning mental illness, especially schizophrenia, society often causes more problems than normal, especially family members. By no fault of their own, the family is crippled in their ability to care for their family member because they do not know how to help them. It is very important families, communities, churches etc. become more educated.

<u>Commonly Asked Questions About Schizophrenia</u>

What is schizophrenia?

- Schizophrenia is a chronic and severe mental disorder which affects how a person thinks, feels, and behaves with very disabling symptoms. Some people with schizophrenia may even seem to have lost touch with reality. (Schizophrenia)

What are some statistics of schizophrenia?

- Schizophrenia is one of the top fifteen leading causes of disability worldwide. Experts estimate almost 1.2 percent (approximately 3.2 million) of the United States population suffers from schizophrenia. Approximately half of individuals with schizophrenia may suffer from another mental disorder, such as depression or bipolar disorder.

What are symptoms of schizophrenia?

- Symptoms of schizophrenia usually become visible in teenagers between ages 16 and 30. In very rare cases, children can be diagnosed with schizophrenia, however, all other child disorders should be ruled out first. It is also rare for adults older than 45 years of age to be diagnosed.

- In <u>Signs and Symptoms of Schizophrenia (NIMH)</u> some symptoms of schizophrenia include:

  o **Thought disorders** are unusual or dysfunctional ways of thinking. One form of a thought disorder is called "disorganized thinking." This is when a person has trouble organizing his or her thoughts or connecting them logically. They may talk in a confusing way hard to understand by others. Another form is called "thought blocking." This is when a person stops speaking abruptly in the middle of a thought.

  o **Hallucinations** are a perception which involves hearing, seeing, smelling, tasting, or feeling things that are not actually there. The most common hallucinations in schizophrenia are auditory hallucinations—hallucinations of sounds and voices. Voices can either speak to

...

the schizophrenia sufferer in second-person voices (you) or third person about him voices (he). Voices can be highly distressing, especially if they involve threats or abuse, or if they are loud and incessant. On the other hand, some voices—such as the voices of old acquaintances, dead ancestors, or 'guardian angels'—can be a source of comfort and reassurance rather than of distress. (Burton, N), (Understanding Voices)

- o **Delusions** are thought disorders (unusual or dysfunctional ways of thinking) defined as strongly held beliefs which are not amenable to logic or persuasion and are out of keeping with their holder's background. Although delusions need not necessarily be false, the process by which they are arrived at is usually bizarre and illogical. In schizophrenia, delusions are most often unprovoked beliefs of being persecuted or controlled, although they can also follow a number of other themes. (Burton, N)

- o **Movement disorders** (agitated body movements) may appear as agitated body movements. A person with a movement

...

disorder may repeat certain motions over and over. In the other extreme, a person may become catatonic. Catatonia is a state in which a person does not move and does not respond to others. Catatonia was more common when treatment for schizophrenia was not available, however, it is rare today.

- o **Flat affect** is a reduced expression of emotions, facial expression or voice tone. At times a person's face does not move or they talk in a dull or monotonous voice.
- o Reduced feelings of pleasure in everyday life.
- o Difficulty beginning and completing activities.
- o Problems with **working memory** (the ability to use information immediately after learning it)?

What types of treatment are available?

- In <u>Common Treatments of Schizophrenia (MAYO Clinic)</u> it is noted that Schizophrenia requires lifelong treatment, even when symptoms have subsided. Treatment with medications and psychosocial therapy can help manage the condition. In some cases, hospitalization may be needed. Treatments include…

o **Medications** are the cornerstone of schizophrenia treatment, and antipsychotic medications are the most commonly prescribed drugs. They're thought to control symptoms by affecting the brain neurotransmitter dopamine.

o **Individual therapy.** Psychotherapy may help to normalize thought patterns. Also, learning to cope with stress and identify early warning signs of relapse can help people with schizophrenia manage their illness.

o **Social skills training.** This focuses on improving communication and social interactions and improving the ability to participate in daily activities.

o **Family therapy.** This provides support and education to families dealing with schizophrenia.

o **Vocational rehabilitation and supported employment.** This focuses on helping people with schizophrenia prepare for, find and keep jobs.

What can families do to help a family member suffering with schizophrenia?

...

o Caring for and supporting a loved one with schizophrenia is a difficult on-taking, however it can be done with proper education. It can be difficult to know how to respond to someone who makes strange or clearly false statements.

o It is important to understand schizophrenia as a biological illness which effects the client's cognitive ability to reason logically.

o You can help find treatment and encourage them to stay in treatment.

o Remember their beliefs or hallucinations seem very real to them; tell them you acknowledge that everyone has the right to see things their own way.

o Be respectful, supportive, and kind without tolerating dangerous or inappropriate behavior.

o Check to see if there are any support groups in your area.

How do Christian Therapists incorporate Christian ideals when working with clients diagnosed with schizophrenia?

Christian Mental Health Providers help clients understand that religion and spirituality play an important part in many people's experiences with schizophrenia. For some sufferers' religious delusions or intense religiously based irrational thinking may be a component of their symptoms.

- o Some may believe they have been sent by God as a great prophet, or, they are being persecuted because of their sins, their family's sins or the sins of the world...like Jesus.

- o For others religion and spirituality play an important role in their recovery process. They may find their spiritual beliefs and practices help them to make sense of the world in a way they could not when suffering from psychotic delusions.

- o Membership of a supportive faith community provides vital fellowship when faced with the everyday problems of living with a serious mental health condition.

Suicidal thoughts and behavior

- Suicidal thoughts and behavior are common among people with schizophrenia. If you have a loved one who is in danger of attempting suicide or has made a

...

suicide attempt, make sure someone stays with the person. Call 911 or your local emergency number immediately. Or, if you think you can do so safely, take the person to the nearest hospital emergency room. (Understanding Voices)

REFERENCES

Banks, G., (2000). Sharing Christ with Black Muslims
https://www.amazon.com/Sharing-Christ-Black-Muslims-introduction/dp/B0006F5YOG

Burton, N., (2012). Schizophrenia: Coping with Delusions and Hallucinations. Retrieved from
https://www.psychologytoday.com/us/blog/hide-and-seek/201208/schizophrenia-coping-delusions-and-hallucinations (with written permission to use)

Living with Schizophrenia UK. (2017). Understanding Voices. Retrieved from
https://www.livingwithschizophreniauk.org/information-sheets/understanding-voice-hearing/ (with written permission to use)

MAYO Clinic. (2018). Common Treatments of Schizophrenia. Retrieved from
https://www.mayoclinic.org/diseases-conditions/schizophrenia/diagnosis-treatment/drc-20354449 (with written permission to use)

Mental Health America. (2018). Schizophrenia. Retrieved from
https://www.mhanational.org/conditions/schizophrenia#intro _ (with written permission to use)

National Institute of Mental Health (n.d.). Burden of Schizophrenia. Retrieved from
https://www.nimh.nih.gov/health/statistics/schizophrenia.shtml#part_154883 (with written permission to use)

National Institute of Mental Health (n.d.). Signs and Symptoms of Schizophrenia. Retrieved from

...

https://www.nimh.nih.gov/health/topics/schizophrenia/index.shtml (with written permission to use)

THE STORY OF WADE REVIEWS

I enjoyed reading about Wade's journey. I can't say that I personally identify with Wade's struggles, but I have dealt with people close to me who suffer from schizophrenia and bipolar disorder. So I recognize the symptoms and mannerisms Dr. AudreyAnn portrayed in her book . It was my intent to read *The Story of Wade* over a period of 4 days. But just like *Saved By Grace* I was unable to pull myself away from the story. Simply amazing!!!
Mark A. Webb, Sr. BMCS(SW), USNR-TAR (Retired) - Virginia

****

We are all plagued with demons/voices from our past, tempting us to throw away the future God has planned for us. *The Story of Wade* is a wonderful reminder that we're never beyond His mercy and grace. Well written, easy to read and very relevant for this day and age.

R.M. Freeman – Virginia

****

As I read the story of Wade, I found it very captivating, thought provoking, heart wrenching, yet, inspiring. The author captured the essence of the torment that Wade may have been facing from within. It was very hard to put the book down because each chapter gave me a glimpse of Wade and why 'The Voices' in his head stirred up so many emotions. This book gives the reader an inside glimpse of mental illness and the individual's struggles. It also broadens our understanding of this illness, it helps us to look into the heart and soul of the person with the illness and it gives us

...

hope by providing resources for the individual and anyone that is affected by this disease/disorder.

Ismay Gordon, Teacher – Texas

****

A must read and an absolute true page turner. The insight of this book provides great guidance on how to listen to people and notice the warning signs of mental illness. The brilliance of the therapist bringing Wade to become whole, and seeing how Wade even helped her become stronger, was magnificently illustrated! *The Story of* Wade is truly a story of hope, a reminder to never give up on people, finding true love and the power of forgiveness and restoration! Once you read this book, you will have no other choice but to recommend it to others! Simply life changing!!!!!

Anthony R. Sanders, Pastor – Author of 90 Days: A Journey Between You and God

www.ingramcontent.com/pod-product-compliance
Lightning Source LLC
Chambersburg PA
CBHW052027020726
47501CB00004B/1285